DEATH FINDS A WAY:
A JANIE RILEY MYSTERY

By Lorine McGinnis Schulze

This book is a work of fiction. Names, characters, and events are a product of the author's imagination and any resemblance to actual individuals or events is coincidental. Any places and locales that exist are used fictitiously.

Acknowledgements

Thanks goes to my husband Brian Massey for his support, encouragement, and participation in brainstorming sessions.

To my son Tyler Schulze and daughter Judy Tellers who read my manuscript and offered helpful suggestions.

To Douglas Fehlen who gave so generously of his time and expertise to offer invaluable suggestions.

Thank you also to Lisa Alzo, Diana Bobo, Terri O'Connell, and Mark Olsen for insightful comments, and to Anne Roach for sharing her impressive knowledge of the horticulture of Salt Lake City

1

Sixteen-year-old Katie shivered in the cool morning air and pulled her woolen cloak tighter as she nudged her brother. Tendrils of glossy blue-back hair escaped from her hood and she impatiently pushed them back. "Joey!" a soft cry escaped Katie's lips. "Look! That must be New York!" Brother and sister were standing on the deck of the ship that had brought them from Queenstown Ireland. The bow plunged through the murky water and the shoreline loomed closer. "Finally," muttered Joey, "I can hardly wait to get off this damn thing and on to solid ground again!"

The passage had not been an easy one. Joey had been ill for most of the voyage across the Atlantic. They were both happy to be on deck where the smell of salt air filled their nostrils. Being stuck below in steerage was miserable. Katie wasn't sure she would ever get the smell of urine, vomit, and other body waste out of her nostrils. Babies with colic screamed long into the night, hungry children cried for hours, and passengers who were sick moaned and retched with horrible gagging noises. Women cried out in fear on hearing the ship groan and creak as its wooden hull protested with every wave that hit. Katie had taken to wrapping her cloak around her ears at night so that the dreadful sounds were muffled.

She shivered again, partially from the cold and partially from nerves. They were starting a new life in a foreign country. She remembered vividly the day Joey came in from the fields and she had to tell him that their beloved ma was gone. Pa had died of the fever just a few months before and their ma had followed not long after.

Now here they were here in a city where they knew no one. Joey had a few pounds to see them through until they could find work but Katie was terrified it would not be enough. She hoped that the emigration agent had been telling the truth when he said jobs were there for the taking in New York City. She prayed she could find a position as a maid or downstairs kitchen girl in a good home, while Joey figured that with his strong muscles and young back he'd work on the docks or help in a stable. He was good with horses and even though he was only 18, no one knew more about gentling or taming a horse than he did.

The cool wind had reddened Katie's cheeks and they felt numb. She was glad the bad weather had finally lifted and she had something to look at besides waves and gray water. The sun was just coming up and Katie imagined she could feel a slight warmth from it already. She could hear the cries of gulls overhead, this sign of land bringing comfort to her.

Joey nudged her. "Katie, look! I think we're coming into the harbor." He pointed to an island on one side, mainland on the other and the narrowing gap of water between them. Their excitement, coupled with apprehension, built. What would happen now? How long would it take to get off the ship, find their baggage, and get on their way? But on their way where? Katie reminded herself that they did not have a place to stay or employment waiting for them.

She saw that they were heading to the island and soon they were anchored. Passengers were told to gather on the deck while officials undertook a quick inspection of their hair and mouths. Joey whispered that these were Health Inspectors checking for disease. Anyone who was found in an unhealthy state would be kept in quarantine. An hour later, the inspection was over and a few sobbing women and young children had been taken away. Katie silently said a grateful thank you for not being one of those rejected.

The ship was once again heading away from the island and Katie could see a large circular building up ahead. When the ship anchored, other officials came on board and began checking each passenger's baggage. More hours passed and Katie felt faint from hunger. The bit of bread and meat she'd eaten at last night's supper was gone from her stomach, and it was now long past their usual breakfast time. Joey kept reassuring her that they were fine, it was almost over and soon they'd be on their way but she was beginning to doubt it.

Finally the exhausted passengers were herded into smaller

boats. She clung tightly to Joey's sleeve, terrified that in the crush of milling bodies they'd be separated. Joey thrust a small piece of bread and some money into her hand "Take this," he whispered fiercely, "and if we get separated, find a spot where carriages come, and wait for me there. I'll find you."

With trembling hands, Katie stuffed the money into the pocket of her full skirt, where it nestled beside the embroidered hanky her ma had given her for her last birthday.

"Joey, I'm scared!" Katie's voice shook slightly.

"It's fine, it's fine, we'll be alright. It's just in case. Eat yer bread now. We don't know how much longer this might take."

The small hunk of bread he thrust under her nose smelled musty but she took it gratefully. She chewed dutifully but could taste nothing, and swallowing was difficult with her dry throat.

The barge they were on plunged through the water for a few more minutes then tied up to a dock. They were ushered off and into the building she'd seen from the ship. Passengers were beginning to stream in, and the noise level increased as men began asking where they were to go next and mothers comforted tired and cranky children.

Officials pointed them to various lines where passengers were examined carefully. The bewildered passengers had to open their mouths and show their tongue. Throats were peered down, ears looked at, foreheads felt for fever. This time the inspection was much more thorough and they were asked questions about their health. Several people were herded into another room but she and Joey were waved ahead where it seemed those deemed healthy were gathering.

Soon they found themselves with other confused passengers in a large circular space in the very center of the building. Men sat at long wooden tables and passengers were led there in turn. Katie found herself standing nervously in front of a man who without taking his eyes off the ledger book in front of him barked curtly, "Name!" "Katie Donnelly sir," she replied. He wrote her name quickly in the book.

"Nationality!" Katie hesitated, unsure of what he meant. He glanced up "What country do you belong to girl!"

"Oh. Ireland sir."

"Last place of residence?"

"Sligo, sir." More scribbling in the ledger.

"Destination?" "Do you mean where am I going, sir?" Katie's throat was so dry and she was so nervous she could barely speak.

"Yes, yes, where are you heading or are you staying here in the city?"

"Right here sir with my brother." The official cut her off impatiently. "Fine, that's it, you can go."

"Where do I go next sir?" Katie asked but had no answer as he called out loudly to the next person in line, "You there! Name!"

Katie looked around for Joey and had a moment's panic but then spotted him standing near the wall, trying to get her attention. Dragging her heavy valise, she pushed through the crowds, almost in tears as she was jostled left and right by other immigrants who were frantically trying to get into line so they could be cleared. Joey grabbed her arm and pulled her close. "Jaysus Katie, keep a sharp lookout!"

"Rooms for rent! Clean rooms for rent at reasonable rates!" Katie was shoved from behind as a frantic young man pulling his very pregnant wife, pushed by to get to the waving arm of the man offering rooms for rent. "I need a room! I'll take it!"

"We need a room ourselves, so let's try to find someone else offering them." Joey's voice was urgent.

And with that he was gone, his sturdy frame forcing a path through the cluster of men, women and children milling about. "Keep up with me Katie!" he yelled in his booming voice. Katie struggled along as fast as she could in her full skirt which fell to the floor and even fuller cloak which fell to her calves. Her sturdy boots helped her keep her footing but there were so many people standing, moving, some even sitting wearily on their trunks that she had to keep weaving around them.

Joey stopped in front of a man wearing black trousers, shirt and vest and over all, a dark blue loose-fitting sack coat that was now so popular. On his head was perched a bowler hat and a sign held high that read Boarding House Keeper. For the benefit of those who could not read, he was yelling out the words on his sign.

Slightly out of breath, Joey blurted out, "Here, here, we need a room!"

Turning towards them, the fellow smiled showing yellowed teeth. "And a fine room I have for you."

Soon a price was agreed on for one room that they would share. Joey took a paper with their new address scribbled on it and made his way to the door.

The outside air made Katie shiver violently. She pulled her wool cloak tighter, and raised the hood, noticing as she did that many of the women wore thick gloves to keep their hands warm. All she had was her cloak so she stuffed her shaking hands deeper. Carriages stood waiting and everywhere noise and unfamiliar smells assaulted her senses. Horses whinnied impatiently, men cursed, hawkers shouted, and women called out to their children.

Joey's voice broke through her thoughts. "We have to find the Labor Exchange. One of the Agents inside told me their office is nearby." They set off across the crowded dock. Inside the Exchange building throngs of newly arrived men and women crowded around tables where men sat waiting to hire the strongest and the best workers.

Some thirty minutes later Katie had a position as a kitchen servant for a gentleman and his family. The Agent assured her it was a fine home and the family was a good upstanding one. Luckily there were several openings for dock workers and Joey had been offered a position almost immediately. Katie's worried face prompted Joey to whisper in her ear, "Don't worry little sister, I'll be fine and I can look for a better job elsewhere while working this one."

They spotted a waiting carriage and Joey helped her into it. "Katie girl we're off!" Joey's excitement captured Katie's attention and she smiled for the first time that morning. It was the start of a brand new life and nothing could ruin it for her!

2

"Steven! Steven!" Janie Riley's frantic voice came from the bottom of her bedroom closet. "Have you seen the wheely for my laptop?" Janie's wheely was one of her most-used items. Hers had only the aluminum frame and was so lightweight she could handle it easily. She hurriedly tossed several pairs of dirty socks to one side, and fished around behind plastic tubs stacked against the wall. "I need it for the library but I can't find it anywhere!"

"Well, where did you put it last time you got home from a research trip?" Her husband's calm voice floated down the hall to Janie's ears. Steven was never in a hurry, always seemed unflappable, and was infuriatingly calm whenever she was so stressed out she thought she might break in two. The flight to Salt Lake City was leaving at 7 a.m. from JFK and that meant at minimum a one-hour drive to get there. With all the extra security precautions Janie knew they needed to arrive at least two hours ahead. That meant they had to leave in the next thirty minutes. And she still had to do her makeup.

Janie was looking forward to this research trip. She was hot on the trail of her father's ancestors, and she could hardly wait to get to the microfilm readers and start searching for the birth record of her ancestor Elizabeth Shuart. It had been four years since she'd been to Salt Lake City and it was going to be wonderful to dig into the records again. Finding Elizabeth's birth would give her another generation of her ancestry! Then it would be on to the next record. Her thoughts trailed off as she realized Steven was looming over her, his bulky six-foot frame blocking her light.

"Okay hon, calm down and come out of there. I'll check in the basement and you just concentrate on getting yourself ready to go. It's not a big deal. If I can't find it we'll buy another one!" Steven smiled and shook his head as he ambled off in search of the missing wheely. He'd been married to Janie for fifteen years and still marveled at her inability to remember where she'd put items. Yet she never missed details of what was going on around her, picking up on the smallest change in other people's body language or voices. These changes went over his head completely. He figured part of it was that she'd majored in Psychology in college, a fact she never let him forget. But she had an innate skill for reading people, one that couldn't be explained only by her education. But remembering where she put things was not her forte.

"Found it" Steven called out. Janie heaved a sigh of relief and mentally shook herself, trying to calm down. Flying wasn't her favorite thing and she needed to relax before they got on the plane. Once she got to Salt Lake she'd be in overdrive, up early each day to beat the rush at the library, staying all day with barely a bathroom or lunch break, and not leaving until library staff were ready to close the doors at night. Genealogy research was addictive and exhausting! But Janie loved it and would crank microfilm readers for hours on end, hoping that a clue to her ancestors would be on the next screen, the next crank of the reel.

No time for daydreaming, she reminded herself. She still had her makeup and hair to do. Eyeing herself critically in the bathroom mirror, Janie decided she wasn't bad for a 54 year old. Hazel eyes stared back at her, taking in her shaggy shoulder-length hair which was well maintained and dyed a gorgeous coppery chestnut by her stylist in Delaware. She inspected her face. Overly strong chin and rather large features but all in all not bad.

A spattering of freckles across her nose and skin that luckily was not prone to blemishes gave her a youthful appearance. She was blessed to have only a few wrinkles at the corners of her eyes; probably her oily skin should be thanked for that. Her hair was conscientiously dyed every four weeks so that her natural dark brown color never showed its roots. With practiced strokes, Janie applied her eggplant eye shadow. A bit of cream blush on her cheekbones, lip gloss on her lips and she was almost done. Her feathered cut hair required very little maintenance – a bit of gel and the wind-blown look she favored was complete.

Steven's voice interrupted her thoughts. "Time's up. C'mon Janie, we're outta here!" Zipping up her makeup bag, she tossed it into her waiting carry-on, grabbed her spring jacket and hurried out the front door before Steven could call her a second time.

"Wait!" Janie called out to Steven, "Did you remember to lock up the paintings?" They had dozens of paintings by well-known artists, acquired by Steven in his search for artwork for his wealthy clients. He specialized in 19th century and early 20th century art, and most of the pieces they owned reflected that time period. Steven bought art as an investment but Janie preferred to choose the pieces that appealed to her in some way. They owned a few pieces of artwork such as one by Lucy Angeline Bacon that were worth quite a bit of money and when they went on vacation those were taken off the walls and locked in Steven's secure vault.

"Yep, all taken care of, now let's go." Steven glanced at his watch. Their Limo driver stood patiently with the car door held open. Janie settled herself in the back seat, mentally checking off her list for the third time. Lock all doors and windows. Lock up paintings. Turn water off. Set timers for lights. Unplug all kitchen appliances. Set security alarm. Pack her Epi-Pen in case of an allergic reaction. She knew they'd done all of them but had to run down her list anyway.

Soon they were at the airport and boarding their plane. The flight was uneventful, and after landing in the Salt Lake City Terminal it hadn't taken long to get their luggage from the carousels. Steven left her with their bags while he went off to find where they needed to catch their hotel shuttle.

Checking the watch clipped to the inside of her purse, Janie calculated they'd be checking in to their hotel by noon Utah time. She hated watches and rarely wore one, but for this trip she needed to be careful of her timings, as her son called them. She'd taken her vintage Mickey Mouse watch from the safe and pinned it safely inside her purse. It was a gift from her father given just before he died and was her most prized possession. If she had to take one it might as well be one that made her smile when she looked at it.

While she waited Janie lost herself in another of her favorite activities – people watching. Unlike Steven, Janie could lose herself in observing people's interactions and behavior. She

8

loved to analyze people and thought she'd have made a good psychologist or detective. In fact, genealogy was a lot like detective work. You found a clue that led to other clues, analyzed the information you found, and developed theories that research proved or disproved, until you solved the puzzle.

Looking around, she spotted Steven's Fedora hat headed in her direction. He loved his hats and had quite a selection at home. Today he was wearing his faded brown one, a comfortable favorite that he wore whenever they traveled. With the Fedora, his work boots, khaki casual pants and button shirt, he looked more like Indiana Jones than usual. Janie smiled as she thought of the nickname of Indiana Magnum that her son had given his stepfather because of Steven's Indiana Jones look combined with his love of brightly colored Hawaiian style shirts.

The hot dry heat of Salt Lake City enveloped them as they stepped through the terminal doors to the sidewalk. Crowds of travelers were gathered waiting for their shuttle buses. Janie felt like she was in an oven. It was a lovely day but she wasn't used to such high temperatures. She could feel the moisture being sucked out of her skin and made a mental note to use lots of moisturizer when they arrived at the hotel. Last time they were in Salt Lake City her lips cracked, her hands cracked and she was raw and red for the whole week she was researching. Cranking a microfilm reader was very unpleasant when your hands were cracked and sore.

A sudden commotion made both Janie and Steven turn. Further down the sidewalk Janie spotted an older man with unkempt gray hair hanging limply over a grubby black sweater. Sweat dripped from his forehead. Dirty black jeans were frayed at the hem where they fell over worn black shoes. "Give that back!" The man in black spluttered, grabbing a bulky long black trench coat from the arms of the shuttle driver. Janie watched the man climb the stairs to board the bus for the Red Lion Hotel. Steven took her arm and gently turned her away. "That's none of our business, Janie."

A tattered and dirty gray lunch bag sat on the sidewalk where the old man had stood. The shuttle driver was in his seat and seemed unaware that the bag had been left behind. Ignoring

Steven, Janie walked quickly to the bus, picked up the bag and boarded, then called out "Did someone leave this on the sidewalk?" The few passengers on board looked at her without speaking but the old man in black looked up and nodded his head. Janie smiled and walked towards him. "Wouldn't want you to forget this," she chirped. Without speaking he snatched the bag from her hands and turning away, clutched it tightly to his chest. "Okay, well, there you go," said Janie. Everyone on the bus was staring and she saw the driver's eyes watching her in his rear-view mirror. Janie quickly mumbled an apology for delaying them and left the bus.

Steven gave her a look and shook his head when she returned. "Why do you do it?" he asked, without expecting an answer. At that moment their shuttle arrived and Janie held her tongue. Soon they were bouncing along the highway leading into the city, mercifully cooled by the air conditioning blasting from the front vents.

3

The shuttle bus pulled into the semi-circular drive of their hotel and Janie and Steven hopped out. Passing through the wide front doors to the reception desk they checked in, then they were in the elevators to their room on the 6th floor.

Janie decided to drop her suitcase, rinse her face, put on her lipstick and gloss, grab her research bag, and head to the library. Her comfortable airplane travel clothes would do nicely for a library visit and she could unpack later. Tossing her suitcase on the bed, she frantically searched for her favorite red sandals and her research sweater, a charcoal long sleeve cardigan. She needed that sweater. It was soft and comfortable and just heavy enough to ward off chilly air-conditioning. And she loved her sandals even though the strap sometimes slipped off her heel. One of these days she'd have Steven take a look and do something to fix the problem. That slipping strap had caused her to stumble more than once.

"See 'ya later hon. Around 7 okay for you?" Janie kissed Steven's ear as she grabbed her research bag. Steven gave a peck into the air as he settled back on the king size bed with a sigh. His size 11s kicked off, he worked his toes and plumped several pillows under his back and head. "Sure sweetie, that's fine, I'll make reservations for 8 o'clock. Romano's Macaroni Grill tonight?"

Janie was out the door before he finished his sentence. Taking the elevator down to the main floor lobby, Janie walked quickly to the side door that opened to the alley between the hotel and the library. Down the alley to the sidewalk on West Temple Street, another few minutes and she'd be at the front doors of the Family History Library, Mecca for genealogists around the world.

Janie passed through the front doors and smiled at the Family History Library greeter. Shades of Wal-Mart, she thought! The library had both paid staff and volunteers to help visitors. Smiling greeters manned the exit doors and she assumed they were there to be sure no one took microfilm or books outside.

There were a few researchers at the Information Desk across

from her and she could see many more inside the main reading room. She headed to her right towards the elevators. Since the US/Canada Books had been moved from the Main floor to the 3rd, she didn't find it as convenient. Often there were long waits for the elevators but she didn't feel like taking the stairs today. Soon a small group of eager researchers gathered, all of them impatient for an elevator.

The elevators arrived but quickly filled. One was just about to close its doors but Janie saw that she could squeeze on. One of the passengers held the doors open for her and she stepped inside. She nodded her thanks and smiled at him, her eyes taking in his clean cut, yet rumpled look. He wore a long sleeve button down shirt in dark green, blue jeans, hip-length black leather jacket frayed at the cuffs and looking rather faded in spots. *Definitely showing its age,* she thought to herself. Scuffed brown leather boots. Dark brown, almost black hair with a bit of gray in the sideburns curled past his ears in slight waves. His slightly tanned complexion and chiseled features made Janie think he might have Native American ancestry. He stood out from the crowd. Medium height, solid stance, feet planted firmly, legs slightly apart. Steely gray-blue eyes that appeared to take in the entire elevator car with one glance. She noted that he did not carry a research binder or case.

Just as her glance took in his empty hands he shifted his arm exposing a beat-up Mickey Mouse watch. Janie almost laughed out loud, but restrained herself. She wished she could flash her watch at him to see how he would react. He seemed to sense her gaze and turned his head towards her. Janie blushed slightly and silently cursed her size-everyone-up brain. She was always noticing things that were just slightly off kilter and it was not something she could easily switch off.

On the 3rd floor Janie paused, scanning the room before deciding where to park herself. Years of research in libraries had taught her to avoid certain areas and certain people. She didn't want to be near a talker.

Janie walked slowly around the perimeter of the cluster of long work tables, sizing up where empty chairs were and who was sitting near them. The tables held an assortment of researchers. *Such characters,* Janie thought to herself.

At last she spotted an empty chair across from a nicely groomed middle-aged woman. She hadn't spread her books and laptop across the table, in fact she was taking up very little space. Her white hair was well kept, a short bob with bangs set off a delicate face that had very little makeup, just a soft coral lipstick. She wore a flowered blouse in muted lilac, turquoise and cream that Janie thought suited her pale complexion very well. A gray sweater and black dress pants completed the look which was one of simple good taste. Janie noted with envy the Perlina purse at the woman's side. An expensive leather Bosca briefcase sat at the stranger's feet. A pair of tortoise brown Gucci reading glasses sat perched on the end of a delicate nose and completed the look.

The woman barely glanced up as Janie pulled out the chair across the table. She appeared engrossed in her work, which suited Janie. After arranging her laptop, notepad and pens on the table, Janie attached her laptop cable and wound it around the table leg before locking it. Not perfect but probably enough to foil thieves since anyone wanting to steal it would have to lift the long table where at least ten other people were sitting. Now she was free to find the books she needed for her search.

A short time later, and with a barely suppressed yawn, Janie leaned back in her chair and stretched. She was getting tired and decided she'd spent enough time today going through books. Time to find a microfilm reader. Janie knew Steven thought it was ridiculous, but she had requirements for a reader. It could not be near the windows or the main open space where all the tables and computers were. That was too bright for her. She didn't like one too far down the row because that meant she had to fight her way down between the two rows of chairs that sat, back to back in each row. The chairs were often pushed out so far you could barely walk down the aisle. She hated pushing by everyone and apologizing every time she bumped into a chair.

Looking up as she stood to pack up her laptop and notebooks, she realized that the room was a bit emptier. The woman with the Perlina purse was gone. Quickly Janie hitched her purse strap over one shoulder, grabbed her computer bag and headed for the elevators and the next floor down.

After finding a reader that suited her, Janie dumped her notepad and laptop case on the study carrel to mark it as taken. She soon had her laptop safely fastened to the desk, and then she headed for the microfilm reel drawers. She'd already noted the film numbers from the online catalogue when she was at home so all she had to do was find the right row, the right drawer, and then the correct films.

She hurried back with the films she needed. To her surprise, the nicely groomed woman from the third floor worktable was at the reader beside Janie. She didn't look up from her work and Janie slipped quietly into the chair beside her. Fumbling with the microfilm box, Janie stood to begin the task of starting the reel. A gasp from beside her made Janie turn. Her neighbor was staring open-mouthed at her reader screen with a frown on her face. Observant as ever, Janie noticed the film was a page from a New York newspaper. She smiled and turned away, figuring the woman had discovered something pretty exciting in her family tree.

On her second trip to return her completed films Janie noticed someone watching her. It started as an odd tingly feeling on the back of her neck. She turned quickly and saw someone, a man, move rather quickly around the end of the row and out of sight. A few seconds later she caught a glimpse of a man in dark clothing but when she turned towards him he looked away, opened a microfilm drawer, and began pawing through the boxes inside. She stared. He looked vaguely familiar.

An egg-shaped head atop which was stringy gray hair that fell to his shirt collar. A threadbare black sweater, blue collar of his shirt showing. Grungy black jeans frayed at the hem. He continued pawing through the microfilm boxes and she noted beads of sweat on his unshaven cheeks. Sweat! It was the man from the Airport. She knew she'd seen him before. He seemed aware that she was staring and turned his back, blocking her view.

Janie felt slightly shaken but knew Steven would say she was making a mountain out of a molehill by assuming that something that was almost certainly a coincidence was sinister. The man had a right to be in the library, just as she did. After all hundreds of genealogists walked through the doors every day to research their ancestors. It was also a good bet that there were genealogists on almost every flight into Salt Lake City.

4

An hour passed before Janie decided she needed a break. It was time to re-energize with a snack and a bottle of water from the vending machines in the Snack Room on the Main Floor. The sun was bright as Janie exited through the front doors. It would be nice to sit on the walls of the flower gardens outside.

The woman who had the reader next to her was sitting alone in the shade along one edge of the flower garden. Janie made her way across the courtyard then seated herself a few feet away. She smiled when the woman glanced at her. "What a lovely day," Janie chirped brightly. She never had trouble talking to strangers and they almost always responded agreeably to her overtures.

Her neighbor gave a polite smile and murmured in agreement. She turned back to studying her half-eaten apple with apparent fascination. Janie took the hint and sat quietly, sipping her bottled water and enjoying an egg salad sandwich on sourdough.

Gathering her sandwich wrapper and empty water bottle Janie walked to the sidewalk and tossed them into the trashcan. As she turned to go back, she noticed the same man she'd seen earlier. He was loitering behind a tree, looking at the spot where she'd been sitting. Was he watching the woman with the apple? With a rapid bird like twist of his neck, he spun towards Janie, then shuffled rapidly down the street. *Boy, this is getting weirder,* she thought. Steven would have shaken his head over what he called her overactive imagination. But she'd been proven right more times than not, and she'd learned over the years to trust her instincts. Her little voice was telling her something was definitely going on.

Sighing, she headed back to the microfilm room. She didn't have a lot of time left today and she wanted desperately to make progress on the search for Elizabeth. Her neighbor was back at her microfilm reader and seemed intent on the film she was viewing. Janie finished arranging her laptop on her cubicle. She was engrossed in trying to read the spidery handwriting on the document in front of her when she sensed rather than saw a looming shape behind and to her right. Turning her head slightly she saw a tall paunchy man standing menacingly, looming over her desk. "Clarissa, we need to talk!" the man was almost shouting. Janie realized he was speaking to the well-groomed woman beside her.

The woman he called Clarissa turned quickly. "Ken what are you doing here?" Her voice was low but had a hint of alarm. "Go away!"

"We're talking Clarissa and we're talking now! You're not gonna get away with this. I warned you!"

Clarissa tried to shush him. "Ken, be quiet! This isn't the time or place." Her voice was almost a whisper and she was rising, half standing to speak to him. Even in the dim lighting cast by the microfilm readers, Janie could see that his large round face was flushed. His meaty hands were balled into fists, and his posture was that of a man who was ready for a fight. His breathing was heavy and each word was a staccato burst punctuated with a harsh outward breath. "You. Listen. To. Me"

Clarissa was shaking slightly as she pushed at his chest in an effort to move him away from her desk. Janie turned away, realizing that the woman was probably embarrassed, but kept her head turned slightly so that she could still see out of the corner of her eye. Clarissa and the man she called Ken moved off towards the seating area past the Copy Center. Janie registered some kind of logo across the back of his dark polo shirt. She thought the last part said Landscaping Services but they were too far away for her to be sure.

Janie could no longer hear them but she could see from his waving arms and towering stance that the man was angry. They stopped at the entrance where they continued their talk, Ken leaning in now until his face was inches from Clarissa's. He held her elbow and she appeared to be trying to pull away. Finally he released her, turned on his heel and stomped out. A distressed looking Clarissa rushed to the Women's Restroom.

Janie knew that Steven would not approve, but she decided to follow Clarissa to make sure she was okay. As she entered the bathrooms Janie heard sobbing from one of the stalls. Hesitating only a moment, she walked to the stall door, and tapped gently. "Excuse me, I'm the woman who was sitting next to you at the readers. Are you okay? " The crying stopped. She heard sniffling and toilet paper being pulled from the dispenser. The woman in the stall blew her nose and answered in a shaky voice. "Yes, yes I'm fine."

Janie's voice was gentle. "I saw that man rough you up and I wanted to be sure you're not hurt." Silence. More sniffing and suppressed sobs came from behind the locked door. "Yes, really I'm fine. I just need a moment." Janie passed some tissues under the stall door. "Here, that toilet paper isn't very easy on the nose. Use these." They were accepted with a subdued thank you. Janie decided to sit in the lounge at the door and wait. If Clarissa felt like talking, she was a good listener.

A few minutes later the stall door opened and Clarissa emerged. Her eyes were red from crying and she appeared very shaken. After washing her hands and splashing cold water on her face, she joined Janie in the lounge. Janie smiled gently as the woman inspected herself in the mirror. Finally Clarissa spoke. "Thanks for the tissues. I don't usually burst into tears like that." She dabbed gently at her eyes and ran a brush through her hair. With trembling fingers she searched through her purse, took out a lipstick and ran it quickly over her mouth. Words began to tumble from her mouth. "That was my ex. Or soon-to-be-ex. He's not very happy with me right now, but I guess that was kind of obvious wasn't it." She sat down on the couch. "We're in the middle of a nasty divorce and he's being his usual brutish self." Janie's murmured noises of sympathy and agreement seemed to encourage the woman and she continued. "I've had twenty-four years of misery with that man and I'm finally getting him out of my life so you'd think I'd be laughing, not crying! But I'm not crying because we're divorcing, just that he can be so awful."

"Don't worry about it. When someone treats you like that, you're allowed to cry."

Clarissa crumpled the soggy tissues in her hands. "You're very kind. My name's Clarissa, I guess we haven't been properly introduced." Janie grinned and said wryly, "No I guess we haven't. I'm Janie and I don't always go around talking to strangers in the bathroom."

18

"Your phone was ringing." Clarissa's voice greeted Janie. "Darn, I forgot to put it on vibrate!" exclaimed Janie. She reached into her carry bag and checked the number. Steven had called, she better head to the hall or the stairs and call back to find out what he wanted. Setting her phone to vibrate, she gave Clarissa a smile and apologized. "No, it's okay, I wasn't bothered, I just thought maybe you missed an important call," Clarissa was quick to explain.

Janie returned Steven's call then headed back to her microfilm reader. She stopped short. There was that same weird little man dressed all in black, the one who was always sweating. His clothing hung on his gaunt frame and made him appear even more sinister. He was standing very still at the end of the row of readers where she and Clarissa were sitting. The odd thing was that he had nothing in his hands. No film boxes, no reel of film, no notepad or pencil. Janie found herself transfixed by how still he was. Suddenly his egg-shaped head pulled back. He spun around and shuffled off, disappearing down the next row, his jacket flapping with his rapid movements. She saw Clarissa coming out from their row of desks. Odd that the moment Clarissa started down the row, the little man disappeared. But, she reminded herself, we genealogists are a bit of an odd bunch, so I shouldn't be surprised that some weirdo is getting his kicks staring at a nice looking woman like Clarissa.

Back at her reader, Janie settled in for some serious work. Clarissa returned, saying, "Drat, I forgot to put more money on my copy card and had to lose my place in line for the reader-printers. I don't know where my head's at today."

"Been there, done that," agreed Janie. Even though they were speaking quietly, she noticed other researchers giving them annoyed looks. She knew the unspoken rule was talk softly, whisper if possible, and try not to talk at all. "I think we're in trouble," she whispered to Clarissa, with a nod of her head in the direction of one elderly woman who was glaring at them from her cubicle. Janie felt an attack of the giggles coming on and had to swallow several times to not give in to it. She bit her lips and saw Clarissa suppress a small grin at her discomfort.

"Oh dear, I really think I should go," said Janie. "I'm getting a bit giggly and silly and that won't do. I need a nap before supper. It's been a long day and I'm two hours ahead of myself." Janie wasn't sure she was explaining the time zone change properly but Clarissa nodded. "Yes, travel does catch up with you. And I better get back to work before I get fired." Janie looked at her quizzically. "Fired?"

"Yes, this isn't my own family tree I'm working on, it's for a client."

"How wonderful!" Janie was enthusiastic. "Do you live here in Salt Lake then?"

"No, I used to live nearby but moved away after my separation. But money appears not to be an issue for my client and he instructed me to fly here and stay until the research is done." Clarissa smiled then glanced at her Cartier watch. "I mustn't keep you, and I really do need to figure this out. If you're back in the morning I'll look for you, perhaps we can take a morning break together? It's nice to have a bit of company at times."

"Absolutely. I'd like that and I will definitely be here first thing tomorrow. Good night, and I hope you figure out your puzzle." With a smile and a wave, she left, hoping she had time to catch a short nap before Steven came back from his sightseeing.

Tonight they were going to Romano's Macaroni Grill so she chose her platinum capris with a simple cotton sleeveless black top. She was already wearing her silver Pandora Bracelet Steven had given her on their last anniversary. "You about done in there?" Steven called from the bedroom. "Ready," she responded. He was standing at the door waiting patiently, his slender frame tucked into khaki colored jeans and a Hawaiian shirt in bright greens and canary yellows. He rarely wore anything on his feet except work boots but tonight he'd chosen taupe canvas loafers. No jewelry except a simple gold wedding band on his left hand. And of course, one of his Fedoras, this time a summer one, on his slightly balding head. He hated that he was losing his hair but Janie didn't mind in the least.

"Onward and upward," she said cheerfully. "I've got so much to tell you and I'm dying for some Tiramisu."

"I'd like a treat too," said Steven with a leer. "You look fantastic. Any chance we could just stay here and forget about supper?" He moved in for what Janie knew would be a long lingering kiss, but she put a hand on his chest. "Later, I promise. But I'm starving and need to be fed." She gave a fleeting kiss on his lips. He pretended to pout but released her. "Okay I'm a patient guy. I can wait."

The restaurant was almost empty so Janie chose a table that suited her. Her preference was one against the wall in a quiet corner. With a contented sigh Janie settled into her seat and began rearranging the items on the table, then adjusting her silverware. "How was your day Steven?"

"Good," Steven said with a smile as he watched Janie move things around until she was satisfied. "I did a little sight-seeing, wandered around a bit, getting the lay of the land before heading out tomorrow on some serious tourist stuff."

"Are you going to see the big hole in the ground again?" Janie asked with a half-smile. The last time they were in Salt Lake, Steven rented a car and took a tour of the Kennecott Copper Mine, which Janie ever since referred to as the big hole in the ground. She'd stayed behind and done more research at the library, and fully intended not to be dragged along on any sightseeing on this trip either. Machines and industries and things that she considered toys for boys enthralled Steven. He kept reminding her it was the largest copper mine in the world and was ¾ of a mile deep! And why she didn't want to see trucks as big as houses was beyond him.

"Okay okay, yeah I think I'll rent a car and either go to Kennecott or the airplane museum near Ogden. The one we went to a couple of years ago, remember? It was super cool and I really want to see more." They sipped their drinks. As usual it was water for Janie, Coke for Steven. "Sounds good sweetie. I'm going back to the library in the morning, big surprise right?"

"How'd things go today? Did you find what you were looking for?"

"Nah, I have a lot more microfilms to go through," Janie responded, "but I had an interesting day. Some really weird stuff happened." Steven laughed, then settled back in his chair with a huge grin. "You and your overactive imagination. Okay babe, fill me in. I know you're dying to tell me all about it. How many robberies or murders in progress do you think you saw?"

"Steven, it wasn't like that," she protested. Just then their meals appeared, drinks were refilled, and they settled in to their food. Between bites of her meal, Janie regaled Steven with details of the people she'd encountered that afternoon. Steven said little, intent on demolishing his Italian Sausage Pizza. By the time they were done, she'd finished telling him about Clarissa, Clarissa's soon-to-be ex husband, the man in black, and all the other colorful characters she'd noticed in the library. Wiping his mouth, he chuckled. "Sounds like you're in for a full day tomorrow babe. Try not to stumble over any bodies okay?"

"C'mon Steven, that's not fair, it was just that one time. It's not like I make a habit of it!" She started to protest but he reached across the table to take her hand. "Sweetheart, it's okay. I love you. In fact I'd like to show you how much I love you. Ready to go?"

"I really do want Tiramisu before we leave."

"Okay then I'll have hot tea. But I'm holding you to the

promise you made back in the hotel room!" He winked at her and the deal was sealed. After fifteen years of marriage there weren't many surprises anymore. But she had a husband she loved and who adored her. Steven treated her like a princess. His antique business was doing well and supported them in a very comfortable lifestyle. With his rich clients apparently lining up to have Steven find them the perfect Chippendale table, or an exotic, unusual and over-priced work of art, they had no money worries.

"Janie, earth to Janie." Steven's voice interrupted her thoughts. Janie jolted back to the restaurant and the table that had now been cleared. Her Tiramisu was in front of her, and Steven's tea cup was empty. "Oh my gosh, I'm sorry, I was lost in my daydreams."

Steven's indulgent smile told her he was not annoyed. He poured a second cup of tea. "Last one," he told her. "Please finish your dessert. I'm kind of anxious to get back to the hotel to have my after dinner treat." The look he gave her caused a wave of desire rising into her throat and she felt her face flush. Even after fifteen years he excited her as no other man had ever done. Combine that with the love she felt every time she thought about him and you had a marriage she considered made in heaven.

Steven paid and left his usual overgenerous tip. Janie excused herself to visit the restrooms while Steven walked ahead to the entrance doors.

After applying her lip gloss and fluffing her hair, she left, almost colliding outside the women's entrance with someone leaving the men's room. Startled, she pulled back and gave the customary "Oh, sorry". At the same moment she realized she was apologizing to the man from the terminal. He glared at her briefly then turned quickly and scurried away, his long black overcoat flapping slightly behind him. Janie's lips were open in surprise and she could not move. He disappeared out the front door and Janie walked as quickly as she could to where Steven stood waiting patiently. "Steven" she hissed, "Did you see that man?"

"What man?"

"The one who just went past you! Dressed all in black, stringy long gray hair, long overcoat, really weird looking." She was becoming annoyed with Steven's puzzled look. "Steven honestly! You must have seen him, he went right by you!"

"Didn't notice" Steven shrugged.

"He's the guy I was telling you about, the one who was watching me in the library."

"Well, I'd watch you too if you weren't my wife. In fact I do watch you, you're a hot little number, babe."

Janie had no patience for his teasing and his innuendos. "Steven Riley don't make fun of me, this guy is creeping me out!"

He shrugged. "Look it's probably just a co-incidence. Didn't you tell me that you genealogy nuts don't stray far from the library when you're here?" His arm went around her shoulders pulling her in close. "Let's go back to the hotel and I'll give you a nice back rub and help you forget all about that jerk."

Janie allowed herself to be swept along the sidewalk, Steven holding her close to his side for the walk back to their hotel. Eventually she put her arm around his waist and snuggled in, relaxing against him. He smiled and kissed the top of her head. "That's my girl."

Later in their hotel bed Janie replayed the images of the man in black while Steven snored loudly. Their lovemaking had ended an hour ago but she could not sleep. Pulling her pillow over her left ear, Janie turned on her side where finally her fatigue won out over the noise Steven was making.

7

Janie awoke with the beginning of a migraine. The disturbing images of the man in black watching her had interrupted her sleep several times during the night. Steven's loud snoring hadn't helped either, and her body was now rebelling. She recognized the signs. Dull ache over her left eye. Neck tight as a drum.

Waves of nausea caused her stomach to roll. The morning light streaming through the open curtains seemed overly bright, causing her to wince and turn her head away from the glare. The clunk and hum of the air conditioner was an ear-splitting jet airplane to her.

She needed to nip this in the bud before a full-fledged migraine started up or she'd lose an entire day of research. She couldn't bear to look at microfilm when she was feeling like this. Thank goodness for the new pills her doctor had given her, with any luck if she took them now, the headache would ease. Coffee would help too – lots of it.

Pushing back the bed covers she marveled at Steven's ability to sleep. He rarely got up before 9 a.m. which she didn't mind since it gave her a couple of hours of quiet time in the morning. Stumbling to the hotel coffee maker she brewed a pot. She waited impatiently for the coffee to finish, then poured a mug. Usually she loved the smell of coffee in the morning, but this morning it was torture. She felt nauseated from the strong odor. This cup was medicinal, not for taste, so she added two packages of sugar and two containers of cream from the fridge. Gulping the first cup down quickly along with her migraine pill, she continued slowly drinking one cup after the next. In half an hour the pot was empty.

Food. That was the next trick. Get some bland food into her stomach as fast as possible. Ordering from room service was the answer on a day like this. She needed to eat before the migraine hit full force. Room service first, then a quick shower. Hot water might loosen the tightness in her neck although ice was the best solution. An ice pack on the back of her neck always eased the pain. Maybe Steven would get her some ice cubes after he woke up. He was still snoring when she came out of the shower so she'd have to wait a bit but she quickly dressed before room service knocked at the door.

After a hasty breakfast of lukewarm scrambled eggs, toast and more coffee, she felt half-human. The pills were starting to work, and her pounding head was turning into a dull ache. A nap might be the best thing for her right now. If she forced herself to go to the library she'd only make herself sicker and likely end up leaving by lunchtime. She'd already pulled the drapes closed. The darkness was soothing and she knew the pills had kicked in enough to help her sleep. Just a little nap on the couch, then she'd get up and start the day. No sense waiting for those ice cubes since Steven was still asleep.

Janie woke to the sound of the shower. Steven was no longer in bed and the clock on the bedside table read 9 a.m. She'd slept for almost two hours. Stretching, she realized her headache was pretty much gone. Her only symptoms now were a lingering fuzziness as if her brain wasn't quite up to speed. "Hey sweetheart, how come you were sleeping on the couch?" Steven came out of the bathroom, a damp towel wrapped around his waist, his wet hair dripping water on the rug. "Everything okay?"

"Yep, I'm fine." Janie stood up and yawned. "Just a little sleepy that's all, and a bit of a migraine but it's under control now." Steven kissed her good morning. "Can I help? A neck or foot massage?" He knew that a foot massage always put her to sleep and then the migraine often subsided. But Janie shook her head. "No thanks sweetheart. I've already slept and my head feels a lot better."

"That's good. Then how about breakfast? I'm starved! But I guess you've eaten?" He eyed the dirty dishes on the room service tray.

His disappointment was clear. Janie felt guilty about leaving him every day while she pored over microfilm and he did his sightseeing alone. Mustering a smile, she replied in a teasing voice, "No way, you're not avoiding breakfast with me. I'm up for it, so let's go."

A few minutes walk through the hotel to the restaurant and

they were seated in a booth by the window. Both decided on the breakfast buffet and took their place in the lineup. Janie returned to their table first and sat staring outside. Steven's plate was heaped with sausage, bacon, fresh fruit, a muffin, scrambled eggs and hash browns. Watching her nibbling on a piece of dry toast and sipping weak tea, a look of annoyance flashed across his face. "For God's sake Janie, you look like you're waiting for the Inquisition to tear your fingernails out! Go. Get your tail to the library, don't sit here as if you're being punished." More guilt assailed Janie. She tried to apologize, to explain her preoccupation but Steven was not in the mood.

"Hey I understand. You're worried you won't get the perfect microfilm reader in the perfect row, not too near a window, not too far away, but just right. I think I'll start calling you Goldilocks." He wolfed down a sausage and followed it with an angry gulp of his coffee. Janie sat silently, her head turned to look out the window. She didn't feel like a confrontation right now and hoped he would not go on. Suddenly his mood changed. He reached out and laying a hand over hers said in a low voice, "I'm sorry hon. Sometimes I get annoyed at that damned hobby of yours. Hunting for dead people. I'll never understand it. But I know you're anxious so just go, we'll catch up at dinner." The ringing of his cell stopped any comments she might have made. He'd get over it and probably by dinner he'd be his usual easy-going self.

Not wanting to leave things that way, Janie decided on another piece of toast with jam. As she left the buffet area, she was jolted out of her musings by the sight of the man she'd seen several times in the past two days; the one dressed all in black and wearing a long trench coat. He was seated at a table for two and eating breakfast in rapid birdlike nibbles. Janie wondered what he was doing there. She'd seen him get on the shuttle for the Red Lion, so why wasn't he eating breakfast there? She didn't believe in co-incidences but on the other hand, it was true that genealogists in Salt Lake City tended to hang out in the same places.

Steven was still on his cell when she returned to their table. She ate half of her toast before deciding she'd had enough. With a last sip of her tea, she stood, gathered her research notes and laptop, slung her purse over her shoulder, then somehow managed to juggle everything while leaning over to give Steven a quick kiss goodbye. Whoever he was talking to was doing most of the talking and he rolled his eyes, winked at her and gave a little wave. Covering the mouthpiece with his hand, he mouthed, "I'll call you later."

She pantomimed, pointing first to her eye, then her heart and then back at Steven. He smiled and nodded his head. A few minutes later she realized the fresh air was helping to clear her head even more. Even dragging her wheely and laptop awkwardly behind her was enjoyable today. By the time she reached the front doors she was in a much better mood and ready to start her day.

8

The library was crowded and Janie made her way to the 2nd floor as quickly as she could. She hoped there would be a good reader left. She was a lot later arriving than she'd planned and she knew from experience that the readers were claimed pretty fast.

Clarissa was halfway down a middle row of readers and there was an empty carrel beside her. With relief, Janie wound her way down the row, trying to avoid the chairs of other researchers. She recognized the Native American looking man who had held the elevator doors for her the day before. He was sitting in the same row as Clarissa, but on the opposite side. Janie had to pass by his carrel to reach the empty one beside Clarissa and she noticed that he was writing in a small coil flip notepad, the kind you could carry in your pocket. *How odd* she thought, *most of us want larger size paper to write on.* He appeared intent on his work, glancing at the reader image and then scribbling in his notebook. As she walked by she caught a whiff of Old Spice. She smiled slightly thinking how stereotypical that was. Old Spice for a man who looked as capable and steadfast as he did.

Clarissa looked up and smiled as Janie set her laptop on the lower shelf. "I thought maybe you weren't coming today," she whispered.

"Yeah I'm later than I wanted to be," Janie whispered back. "I had to take care of a migraine first."

"Oh, poor you." Clarissa sounded sympathetic. "I rarely get headaches but I know someone who gets migraines and she suffers terribly." Janie settled in to her desk and pulled out her notes. "I'm fine now," she said with a smile. "Time to get cracking on 4th great grandma!" Clarissa also smiled and began sorting her own papers.

"Darn!" She heard Clarissa's exclamation. A few loose papers had fluttered to the floor and landed almost under Janie's feet. As she bent to pick them up Janie saw they were copies of census records for 1870 and 1880 for New York City. "Thanks," whispered Clarissa, taking the papers from Janie. "Clumsy me!"

Soon Janie was lost in her research, scrolling through screen after screen of records on the films she retrieved from the drawers. Clarissa likewise seemed absorbed, often leaning over to peer closely at her film. A sudden gasp from Clarissa caused Janie to look up. Clarissa was sitting back in her chair, her forehead furrowed, a look of puzzlement on her face. Janie glanced from Clarissa's face to the microfilm reader screen.

It looked like church records or vital statistics to Janie. Clarissa was now leaning forward holding a piece of light yellow paper over the cramped and faded handwriting projected on to the white reading surface of the reader. *Must be pretty early*, mused Janie, *or a very poor quality film*. Every researcher longed for a beautiful legible record written in strong dark handwriting but often what they were faced with was a spidery faded bit of what looked like chicken scratches. Experienced researchers knew that holding light pink or yellow paper over the image display usually helped to make faded writing clearer.

Janie could see that the image Clarissa was struggling to read was a birth record. She could just make out the words State of New York Birth Returns. Janie didn't mean to be nosy, but she was curious and she noticed things that others didn't. Things she looked at seemed to register in her brain without her even thinking about what she was doing. This ability, combined with her intuition, was both a curse and a blessing.

Clarissa was now scribbling madly on her lined notepad. She seemed excited at whatever she'd found. Janie wished she could have such an exciting discovery on her lines! Fumbling in her purse, Clarissa pulled out her phone and stood quickly, then walked rapidly down the row of readers towards the entrance. Janie wondered idly what on earth Clarissa had found that was so exciting she had to phone someone about it. She'd also left her reader lamp on, and that seemed completely out of character to Janie. Every time Clarissa left her reader she'd followed the library's printed request that patrons turn the lamps off when the reader was unattended.

Peering over the top of her carrel, Janie saw that Clarissa was nowhere in sight. *Just a little peek*, she thought. Standing, she leaned closer to Clarissa's reader to see what was on the screen.

It was a page of births in New York City for May 1880. There were several entries but Janie didn't want to risk Clarissa seeing her being so curious, so she quickly sat down again.

9

The ringing of the phone surprised him. It was his private cell phone, the one he only used for family and close friends, and they rarely called.

"Yes, who's calling?" Silence at the other end of the line. Then a clear yet tentative voice came through. "It's Clarissa Jones, the genealogist you hired to research your family tree."

"Ah yes, what can I do for you Clarissa?" He'd forgotten he gave her this number, and briefly wondered what she wanted. Clarissa continued, "I've just discovered something rather odd, yet possibly quite exciting, about your third great-grandfather. I wasn't sure if I should divert my attention to this new development and wanted to check with you."

"Tell me what you found," came the response. Distracted by other tasks, he found himself tuning her out. It was likely nothing, all he had to do was half listen, murmur in the appropriate breaks in her monolog and then tell her to go ahead. However as she continued her explanation of her findings, he felt a growing apprehension. He listened attentively, his concern causing him slight indigestion. He reached absently for the bottle of antacids in his bottom drawer, took a swig and placed the bottle down carefully on his desk. She certainly had his attention now.

He could tell from her rapid speech that she wanted to track down this new find. His mind was spinning. He felt frozen, sluggish. He simply could not comprehend how what she was telling him was possible. "Clarissa," he interrupted her, "this is quite amazing, exciting really, and I do want you to continue following this lead. However, I must ask you not to mention it to anyone else until we have all the facts, until we know for sure. Can I count on your discretion in this matter? Of course you must go ahead, that's not a problem, just keep track of your hours and bill me whenever you wish."

Her pleased voice told him he had given the response she hoped to hear. "Oh of course, I never discuss a client's work with other people. I'm very excited about this, I think we can find out quite a bit!"

He interrupted again. "Very good then. Clarissa, I'm sorry to cut you short but I have an appointment and must leave now. Can we talk again in a few days?"

"Perfect," came the reply. "I'll call you by the end of the week. Goodbye now and thank you." Hanging up, he rose immediately from his chair. He walked slowly to his office door and depressed the lock button. He needed time to think. This was something he'd never expected. He must plan, must think about what this new development meant.

Clarissa's excitement was evident when she returned to her reader. Her face was slightly flushed and she was breathing quickly. Janie's curiosity grew. Quickly Clarissa copied an entry from the document of birth registers on her reader, then removed the film from the microfilm reader, being careful not to lose her place. Off she went, probably to the copy room Janie thought.

Janie heard several muffled squeaks and quick inhalations from the next carrel throughout the next two hours. At one point a soft "Oh my!" escaped her neighbor's lips. Janie knew she should keep her eyes on her own screen. But her curiosity was killing her! Purposefully she leaned back, stretched her arms high and managed to squeeze out a yawn, knowing Clarissa could see and hear her. Clarissa gave a quick glance and Janie, alert as ever, seized the opportunity to whisper to her neighbor, "Gosh, I think I need a break. Care to join me?"

Clarissa shook her head. "No, thank you. I've got something I want to check out." *Darn!* Janie thought, *That little ruse didn't work. And now I'm stuck having to take a break whether I want to or not.* She headed for the bathroom where she had a couple of sips of water from the fountain, did one lap around the room then back to her microfilm reader. *Maybe I should take a walk,* she thought. *It might do me good to clear my head.*

With that in mind, Janie made sure her laptop was secure, then took her sweater and purse and headed outside. A quick walk around Temple Square might be just the tonic she needed. She joined two women waiting at the crosswalk to head across the street to the iron gates. There was nothing more peaceful than the walled courtyard that was Temple Square. It took up two city blocks, all of it surrounded by fifteen foot high plastered adobe brick walls. There were hundreds of beautiful flowers. Janie knew the gardens were redesigned every year and she marveled at the creativity of the designers. She wanted to wander the immaculate gardens and take her time looking at the flowers. Everywhere she looked she saw gorgeous clumps of blue-violet columbine, white gerbera daisies, pink astilbe and other flowers she couldn't identify. Hostas provided a green relief against the riot of colors.

The heart of Temple Square was the Salt Lake Temple, which visitors could not enter. But Janie loved standing outside looking up at the imposing neo-gothic structure that had taken forty years to build. Janie had never seen a city as clean as Salt Lake, and she was always impressed by the lack of trash littering the streets. Soon she spotted an empty bench and decided to relax for a few minutes before heading back to the library. She closed her eyes, enjoying the smells of summer, trees, flowers, and earth.

A prickling feeling on the back of her neck caused Janie to tense. She was being watched, she could sense it. Opening her eyes she surveyed the grounds without turning her head. Nothing seemed out of the ordinary. Yawning, she stretched her arms high, bent forward, sat back up, swayed from side to side then stood and twisted at the waist to her left, as if stretching her muscles. There. He was standing between the Tabernacle and the Temple. It was the little bird-like man dressed in black. And he was definitely watching her. Before she could think what to do, he flapped his arms twice and fled, scurrying towards the South gates. Janie watched him go, and debated whether or not to follow but decided against it. Instead she gathered her belongings and headed back to the library, thinking about her latest encounter.

Clarissa was back with three new boxes of film by the time Janie returned. She seemed engrossed in her work. After several hours Clarissa turned off her reader lamp, took her purse and left. Janie glanced at her watch. She really did need to eat something. Stacking her papers and turning off her reader lamp, she checked that her laptop was securely fastened to the desk then looped her purse over her shoulder and walked to the elevators. If it were still a nice day she'd eat outside.

The day was sunny, hot and perfect for sitting in the courtyard. She spotted Clarissa sitting with her face to the sun, eyes closed. A bottle of water and a sandwich sat unopened in her lap. Janie wasn't sure if Clarissa wanted to talk but took a chance. "Hi, mind if I sit here?" she asked. Clarissa shaded her eyes with her hand and opened them. There was no hesitation in her voice as she responded to Janie's question. "Sure, I could use some company."

Over the next twenty minutes they chatted about Clarissa's upcoming divorce, their families and what brought them to Salt Lake City. Clarissa seemed a lost soul to Janie, and she confided that she had no family, having lost both her parents when she was nineteen. She was an only child and completely alone in the world. Without any marketable skills, she'd been forced to work in several low-paying jobs, none of which were stepping stones to a successful career.

Janie shared her own story. When she was sixteen her father was murdered. To add to the shock of his death she was left with a mother who was self-centered and aloof. That was when her beloved grandmother came to her rescue, taking Janie under her wing and acting as a warm and loving mother figure. Clarissa expressed her sympathy for Janie, then continued. When she was thirty years old she met Ken and fell under his spell. With his successful landscaping business and phony charm, he wooed and won her in no time. It hadn't taken long for her to realize that he was a very different person than she'd thought. Their marriage had been hell and Clarissa had spent the past twenty-four years putting up with Ken's wandering ways and violent temper. She'd been too afraid to leave him. "I feel like such an idiot, I don't know why I didn't leave him long ago" Clarissa frowned as she relayed her annoyance with herself to Janie.

Janie shook her head. "You can't blame yourself. He took advantage of you and he used power and money to control you. I was in a similar type of situation myself for ten years. Believe me you can't waste your time with what might have been, should have been, or could have been. It is what it is, it was what it was, and now it's time to put it behind you and move on." Clarissa was listening intently. "I'm excited for you," continued Janie. "You have a whole new life ahead of you and one that you've created. It's yours. You own it. So don't give one second of your time or energy to recriminations."

Clarissa's voice was quiet. "How did you manage to leave? Where did you find the strength?"

"I did it for my son. I knew I couldn't let him grow up with that man, experiencing the kind of dread I went through every day. And I was afraid he might hurt him. He was always threatening to kill himself and take us with him." Clarissa gasped, "Oh that's horrible!"

"It's okay," Janie reassured her. "It's in the past. I came to my senses. I made a decision, a very good one and long overdue, and I left. Now I'm married to a wonderful man and have a great life. I've never looked back. And that's why I'm excited for you, because you are going to have the same thing." Clarissa nodded her head.

"Do you have children?" Janie's question came during a pause. Moisture welled up in Clarissa's eyes. "Oh my goodness look at me! I'm getting so emotional. No we don't have children and I'm so grateful for that but at the same time it's one of the biggest regrets of my life. Ken never wanted children so it just never happened. And now it's too late and I've wasted the last twenty-four years of my life because I was an idiot and didn't have the courage to leave him."

"No you weren't" said Janie forcefully. She shook her head. "We often stick things out because we think they'll get better or we can't figure out how to make a change, but that doesn't mean you wasted those years or that you were stupid. Besides, the past is the past, and now you've taken the step and you're on track to start a whole new life for yourself."

Clarissa nodded her head and confided that she'd finally been strong enough to leave Ken about ten months ago. Before that she'd been too afraid to try to make it on her own. "The thing that helped me was a great-aunt died - my grandmother's sister. I never knew her, she lived in England but she never married and had no heirs. So she left everything to me. It wasn't much but it was enough for me to buy a condo in Colorado. I'd already started my genealogy research business and knew I could make it on my own. And now I have a client who's willing to pay my fees. I even get to stay at the Peery while I'm in Salt Lake, courtesy of his generosity."

Janie explained that she was researching a challenging ancestor. Her father often spoke of his wish to know where the family came from, and after his sudden death, Janie vowed to find the answer. Clarissa nodded and murmured sympathetically.

Before heading back upstairs, Janie took a few moments to call Steven. After making arrangements to meet at the hotel around 7 o'clock, she made her way to the elevators. Waiting with a crowd of other researchers, Janie considered taking the stairs. Just as she was about to do so, the elevators dinged and the doors opened. Stepping back to allow passengers to leave the elevators caused her to collide with whoever was behind her. *Sheesh,* she thought, *talk about standing too close!* She turned to apologize, and as she did so, someone getting off the elevators brushed against her. She hated that! Good grief, could they not see her? Was she invisible? Then she noticed the long black trench coat and realized it was the strange man from the terminal, the one she'd also seen in the library, the man she thought was watching either her or Clarissa.

"Ma'am, excuse me. Excuse me?" Janie realized she was blocking other researchers from accessing the elevator. Flustered, she moved aside and let the stream of people pass by. By the time they had entered the elevator, she could no longer see the man in black. A second elevator arrived and Janie reluctantly entered. Coincidence she wondered? Or something more?

11

The next few hours passed too quickly. Janie's search for Elizabeth Shuart's birth record had not been successful so far, and she was bleary-eyed from straining to see the microfilmed records. Yawning, she stood up from her chair and did a few bends over the back of it. Sometimes that relieved the kinks in her back. Clarissa was nowhere in sight but her laptop and water bottle were still at her carrel so presumably she was still in the building.

Janie still had an hour before she had to meet Steven so decided she could do one, maybe two more reels of film. Absorbed in checking her scribbled film number against the signs for the microfilm drawers, she almost collided with a good-looking man emerging from another row. Her nose registered expensive cologne as her eyes took in his designer jeans, Ralph Lauren tee, expensive windbreaker, and tennis shoes. A Breitling Chronomat Evolution watch in gold and silver showed just below his left sleeve. Janie was impressed. She knew how much a Breitling men's watch cost because Steven had in some wild moment, actually considered buying one last year.

As he walked, the man was intently studying something in his hand. Janie assumed it was a list of film numbers but when he spotted her he hastily shoved it out of sight into his pocket. She realized it was a photograph of a person but she couldn't tell if it was a man or a woman. Barely glancing at her, he passed by, leaving a trail of expensive men's cologne in his wake.

Janie turned to watch him as he moved quickly away. Tall. Wavy black hair, well groomed. He was well built and moved with an air of confidence. A few rows away from her, he stopped, took the photo out of his pocket and once again studied it. He appeared to be scanning the open area microfilm reader area. He must be looking for someone thought Janie. How odd.

She settled in to view her films until it was time to meet Steven. The library didn't close until 9 p.m. so if they had a quick bite somewhere nearby she could come back and finish up the reel of church records she had on her reader. You weren't supposed to tie up readers if you weren't using them but she planned to leave her microfilm on the reel and scatter a few papers around on the carrel. The attendants came along every so often to turn off lamps and to clear away unattended readers but leaving her things would make them think she was just getting more films. A tiny twinge of guilt flashed through her mind but she pushed it away. There were lots of available readers for others to use, it wasn't like she was hogging the only one.

Her purse lay on the back of her chair and she looped it over her shoulder while tucking her laptop under one arm and taking the wheely in her other hand. Her leather research bag dangled from one finger as she attempted to push her chair back in with her hip. A smiling attendant came to her rescue and placed the chair neatly in front of the reader. Janie smiled her thanks. She whispered a goodbye to Clarissa who was standing at her reader changing films, then turned to go. Immediately her attention was caught by a man standing two rows away peering over the top of the microfilm readers in their direction. He was looking down as if studying something in his hand or in the carrel, then looking their way. She was pretty sure it was the man with the photo, the one who left a trail of expensive cologne in his wake. It wasn't exactly bright daylight in the reader area so she could be mistaken.

"Clarissa, do you know that guy?" She pointed in his direction but by the time Clarissa turned to look, he was walking away and was soon lost in a group of people near the end of the row. Clarissa looked puzzled.

"Never mind, just my imagination I guess," Janie whispered sheepishly. "See you after supper if you're still here." With a wave she turned to walk away. Her mind was whirling by the time she got back to the hotel, rinsed her face, freshened her makeup and broke the news to Steven that she planned to go back to the library after supper. Thankfully he was over his pout from breakfast and reassured her he didn't mind.

Supper was a subdued meal at The Olive Garden. Over the house salad and spaghetti, Janie listened to Steven's account of his day at the Kennecott Mines. "They have trucks the size of houses!" he told her enthusiastically. "The pit is so deep you can hardly see the workers at the bottom. Apparently you can see the mine from outer space. It's absolutely amazing!"

Janie listened with half an ear while her mind flitted back and forth between her genealogical puzzle and the strange men she'd seen at the library in the last two days. Birdman, expensive cologne man. What were they up to? Even Mickey Mouse Watch dude seemed a bit off. She knew that Steven would think she was reading too much into what she'd seen but her little voice said otherwise.

By the time they finished their meal, she decided she was too tired to go back to do more research. But she'd left her research notes on her carrel so needed to retrieve them. Steven offered to go with her but she refused. "Thanks but you never know, I might get a renewed burst of energy once I get there and I might decide to stay."

There was still a half hour before closing when she arrived at the library but Janie decided to gather her papers and go back to the hotel. There was no sign of Clarissa and the surface of her reader carrel was empty. Janie noticed a few pieces of paper on the bottom shelf of Clarissa's carrel when she bent down to clear out her own. It was so dark and the bottom shelf extended so far back that it was easy to overlook items. Most likely it was nothing Clarissa needed, but she took the pages just in case. She'd give them to her tomorrow.

12

Another day, another ancestor to find, thought Janie as she stepped into the shower. She was still working on her elusive ancestor. Female ancestors could be challenging to track down. Her only clue to Elizabeth's maiden name was her daughter Lydia's death certificate. Shuit had been recorded as her mother Elizabeth's surname before marriage. It took Janie almost five years to determine that the surname was Shuart, not Shuit, and that it had as many spelling variations as a tree had leaves. But without a birth or marriage record for Elizabeth, Janie was at a standstill. But she was determined to find the records and honor her father's memory.

Toweling herself vigorously, Janie thought about how challenging, yet fun, genealogy research could be. It was a good thing she had a mind for solving puzzles. As she brushed her teeth her mind returned to the happenings in the library over the last few days. The odd little man in black. Clarissa's soon-to-be ex-husband. The Native American looking man. And the latest oddity, the good-looking rich guy with a photo of a woman. Why was he walking around checking people out?

Steven was stirring, waking slowly from sleep as she pulled on comfy black cotton capris, a soft olive green tee and open toed wedge sandals. A hint of makeup came next, just a little khaki green powder lining the upper edge of her eyes, black mascara, sheer lip gloss and a dollop of light rose blusher. She sat on the edge of the bed and patted her husband's leg gently. "Sweetie, I'm almost ready for breakfast. Are you getting up?"

Steven yawned. "Lord it must be early. What time is it?" He groaned when he heard her answer. "Who gets up that early?" Unlike Janie, Steven was not a morning person. But he was a good sport most of the time. "Okay give me ten minutes to shower and get dressed."

After a barely edible breakfast of runny eggs and burnt toast at a nearby diner, Janie rushed off to the library. Steven was on his way to an Airplane Museum at Hill Air Force Base outside of

Salt Lake City so they would not see each other until quite a bit later in the day. He loved airplanes and would most likely spend the entire day there. It was a gorgeous day and Janie almost wished she could forgo the library to enjoy the sun and warmth. But she only had a few more days and could not spare the time. Besides, the library was closed on Sundays, so she could relax and enjoy Salt Lake then.

Once inside the library front doors, Janie headed to the bank of elevators and joined a waiting group of researchers. She heard a ding, and realized the next elevator going up was at the end of the row. Joining the throng of eager researchers moving towards the doors, she hesitated, thinking she might wait for the next one. But it was too late, she found herself propelled gently into the elevator where she was forced to stand in the corner with several people between her position and the doors. She noticed the same good-looking middle-aged man she'd seen on her first day, the one who'd held the elevator for her. He stood out from the crowd and Janie wasn't sure why. It might have been because of his air of confidence that made Janie think he was ex-military. There was something about him that caught your attention. Or at least caught Janie's attention. She recognized that it might be because of her own interest in Native American history. In her research she'd discovered she had a Mohawk ancestor from New York, something that would have pleased her father immensely.

Today the guy was wearing faded jeans, probably the same pair he'd had on two days ago. No leather jacket this time, instead he wore an olive green lightweight multi-pocketed jacket over a short-sleeve gray t-shirt that hugged his muscular body. Janie noticed that he still carried nothing in his hands. Most researchers lugged laptops, binders or notebooks but all she could see was the tip of a small notebook in his jacket pocket. He stared determinedly ahead, eyes focused on the various signs posted on the elevator walls. But Janie felt certain he didn't miss a thing and that he had already sized up the rest of the passengers in the car.

The elevator came to a stop and the passengers exited. It seemed everyone was going to the same floor this morning. Janie rushed off to claim her usual carrel and microfilm reader, heaving a sigh of relief when she saw Clarissa. She was at her usual spot and the reader beside her was still vacant. She was glad she didn't have to find a new spot as she didn't like change.

Today Clarissa was wearing a gorgeous dusty rose cashmere sweater that Janie would have loved to have hanging in her own closet. She looked up and gave a little wave to Janie while sipping from a bottle of water that stood beside her notes. "Good morning Janie," she whispered after putting the bottle down. "Did you come back last night? I left a bit early, had some phone calls to make."

"I was only back to tidy up," came Janie's soft voice. "I decided I was too tired to stay and I want to put in a full day today, really focus on my problem." They both agreed that a day of concentration was in order. Clarissa was hard at work on her client's request and felt she was making great headway on an intriguing puzzle. Janie had several more films of church records to go through. Both women got up to find the microfilms they needed.

A few hours later, Clarissa stretched and leaned over, whispering to Janie, "I'm going to the snack room to get another bottle of water. Do you want anything?" Janie thanked her but said she was fine and Clarissa headed downstairs. A few moments later Janie realized she needed to copy a record she'd found on the film she had in her reader. As she made her way to the copy room she saw Clarissa standing at the elevators. Nearby stood a man staring in Clarissa's direction. He was holding something in his hand but Janie was too far away to see what it was.

As she drew closer she thought she recognized the man she'd seen yesterday, the one wearing expensive clothing. But was it him? This man was wearing a very dirty baseball cap. His cheeks had a faint dark stubble as if he had not shaved and instead of an expensive windbreaker he wore a filthy brown pullover that had several holes, frayed edges and what looked like old food stains on the chest. She edged closer and caught a whiff of expensive cologne. Then she glimpsed a photo in his hand. It was the same man!

Janie was so startled by this transformation that she stood

stock still. He moved to put the photo in his pocket. As he did she caught a flash of reflected light and saw that he still wore the Breitling gold watch on his left wrist. It was definitely the man from yesterday. *What on earth is up with that?* she wondered. She pretended to be absorbed in her reel of film but in reality was trying to see if he was watching Clarissa.

The elevator doors opened, Clarissa stepped inside and the man Janie was watching immediately sat down. He continued staring at the elevator over the top of a magazine he held in his hands. Janie wasn't sure if it was possible that everyone was watching Clarissa. She couldn't stand here much longer or he'd notice her, so she quickly made her copy from the microfilm and headed back to her reader. Clarissa returned a few minutes later with her fresh bottle of water. Janie felt edgy, unable to concentrate, but she forced herself to try to focus on her research. She knew Steven would say she was making too much out of it, that it was just a series of odd co-incidences. But she was almost always proven right although there was the time in St. Lucia when she got it wrong. Terribly wrong.

13

Janie kept her head buried in her reader, struggling to read some very poor handwriting on a church record page from 1778. Eventually she found an empty photocopier and made a copy of the screen, thinking she would ask Clarissa to look it over at lunchtime. She hated asking another researcher to help during their research time, but Janie figured that during a break it would be okay. They'd agreed to stop around lunchtime and get some fresh air.

Sitting outside again in the courtyard, they chatted for a bit about their lives and families. After a few more minutes of idle conversation, Janie pulled out her page of records and they both leaned over to try to decipher that spidery script. The area was crowded today with throngs of genealogists coming and going, and most spots on the garden walls were taken. It seemed everyone wanted to sit outside in the sun. The sun was glaring on the white pages and when Janie turned to create shade with her body, she noticed two things. Standing just inside the library, between the double set of doors, was the man with the photo. Except he wasn't clutching the picture in his hands now. His gaze caught Janie's and he turned quickly on his heel and entered the building.

At almost the same moment, the little birdlike man dressed all in black pushed open the door and shuffled outside into the courtyard. He glanced Janie's way then scurried off down the street. Janie gave her head a shake. She was probably over-reacting. It shouldn't surprise her to see the same people at the library day after day. The genealogy world was a small one in Salt Lake City, with everyone tending to eat at the same restaurants, eager to gulp down a few bites then get back to their research. Just like the ebb and flow of the tide, researchers came, stayed a few days, then left while others surged in for their turn at tracing their family trees. Genealogy was an addictive hobby for those who loved it, and the most boring thing in the world for those who could not see the attraction in hunting for people long dead.

After their lunch, Clarissa stopped at the restroom to freshen up while Janie continued to her microfilm reader. As she rounded the corner, Janie thought she saw someone standing near Clarissa's empty carrel. But as she continued walking, whoever it was suddenly turned and walked the other way. *Maybe Steven is right,* she thought. *Maybe I do have an overactive imagination. But that seems a little odd to me.*

14

Janie chuckled when she heard Clarissa take a deep breath and exclaim, "I don't believe it!" She'd felt that same excitement when making a wonderful discovery in her own research. Peeking over the side of her carrel she saw Clarissa leaning forward and intently studying what looked like a newspaper page. *Back to your own work Janie!* She silently chastised herself and withdrew to her own carrel.

After another half hour of peering at the faded spidery handwriting on her microfilm Janie rubbed her eyes and decided it was time to splash cold water on her face. Clarissa's carrel was empty. Yawning, Janie made her way to the restroom. To her surprise Clarissa was on the sofa just inside the entrance, head back and eyes closed. Her skin had taken on a grayish tinge. "Are you okay Clarissa?" Janie couldn't hide the concern in her voice. Clarissa didn't look well.

With an obvious effort, Clarissa's eyes opened. In a shaky voice she replied, "No. I'm feeling very strange. Quite ill really. I think I need to go back to my room and lie down." With that she started to rise from the sofa but fell back, breathing rapidly. Janie's voice rose in alarm. "Clarissa you're not well! I'm taking you back to your hotel." Telling Clarissa she'd gather her belongings and be right back for her, she left the restroom. Once at the microfilm readers she realized Clarissa's laptop was chained to the desk. Without a key she couldn't remove it but decided it was safe until Clarissa was feeling well enough to come back for it. Her own laptop was also fastened securely and she didn't want to waste time so she'd leave it too. She hastily gathered Clarissa's research notes and stuffed them into her briefcase, then did the same with her own. She could manage both bags and her purse.

Clarissa was sitting upright when Janie returned, sipping water from her bottle and wiping her forehead with a tissue. Her opened purse sat beside her. Beads of sweat dotted her ghostly white face and her lips were an odd gray color. One hand was on her throat and she looked like she was having trouble swallowing. Janie took her arm and helped her stand. "Steady there, I'm going to hail a taxi to get you back to your hotel." Clarissa shook her head feebly in protest. "No, it's not far, we can take the Trax." She clutched her purse and water bottle in one hand. "I'm so thirsty," she said as she took another gulp of her water.

By the time they reached the front doors, Clarissa was leaning heavily on Janie and her gait was unsteady. "I think I'm going to throw up," Clarissa squeaked out the words with a moan. An attendant gave them a quizzical look and asked if everything was okay. Janie nodded and told him her friend was not feeling well. She pulled out her phone. "Maybe I should call for a doctor." Clarissa shook her head. "No, please, I just want to lie down." As they moved down the sidewalk towards the corner to catch the Trax, Janie wondered how on earth she was going to manage. Clarissa was stumbling now and pausing frequently to catch her breath. It was difficult for Janie to juggle two research bags, her purse, and Clarissa. Clarissa seemed barely able to hold her own purse but she clung to it stubbornly. "Where are you staying?" Janie couldn't remember if Clarissa had told her. "Peery," mumbled Clarissa. Her speech was slow and barely audible. Janie had no idea how to get there using the Trax system but she figured they'd just get on at the closest stop and she'd ask the driver.

The light was green at the intersection and they began to cross. Janie was worried that with Clarissa stumbling along slower and slower they would not make it across before the light changed. She was sweating in the oppressive heat and even with her arm around Clarissa's waist she was afraid Clarissa was going to slip from her grasp. A sudden choking sound from Clarissa made Janie peer up at her. Blood was dripping from her nose. Another sound came from Clarissa, a gurgling noise, followed by a moan. Her fingers curled over Janie's arm, clutching frantically. Her pale face stared wide-eyed at Janie and out of her mouth poured copious amounts of foam. She was gasping, choking. One hand went to her chest as she slid to the pavement. Clarissa began to convulse, her head whipping from side to side and her back arching with each convulsion. Nearby pedestrians were staring, but everyone seemed too stunned to move.

Janie went into action. Dropping her bags and purse, she knelt beside Clarissa, trying to turn her on her side and calling out loudly for help.

"Clarissa! Clarissa can you hear me?" she spoke loudly as she tried to keep Clarissa from rolling on her back. Clarissa's eyes rolled back in her head and she seemed completely unaware of her surroundings. *Epilepsy?* wondered Janie. *Is she having an epileptic seizure?* A crowd had gathered around them and people were kneeling near Clarissa in the street. "Keep her head turned." "Don't let her swallow her tongue." "Someone call an ambulance!" Many voices were calling out advice.

A spreading stain seeped around Clarissa's legs and the strong smell of urine filled Janie's nostrils. She realized that the poor woman had lost control of her bladder. Clarissa continued to convulse for several minutes, then stopped as suddenly as she had started. Her lips were covered in foam that dripped down her cheek. She lay limply against Janie's hands which were still trying to hold her on her side. She released her grip and Clarissa slumped on her back like a rag doll. Janie felt under her chin on her neck for a pulse. It was rapid and very faint. Janie wasn't a doctor, had no medical training, but she knew enough to know this wasn't good. As she knelt, feeling helpless, Clarissa's breathing grew more labored. Her chest gave one huge heave and a shuddering gasp then she fell completely still. Janie checked her pulse again. Nothing. Someone knelt on the other side of Clarissa. In desperation Janie looked across to the man kneeling on the other side. "I can't find a pulse!"

He reached out and put two fingers on Clarissa's neck. He shook his head. "I don't feel one either." For a moment Janie was jolted out of her concern for Clarissa by a brief glimpse of a Mickey Mouse watch on his wrist. She looked up and realized it was the same man she'd seen on the elevator in the library.

Just then a commotion arose as paramedics made their way rapidly towards the crowd.

"Okay miss we'll take it from here." With practiced motions a young paramedic moved Janie to one side to check Clarissa's vital signs. A blood pressure cuff was on her arm so fast Janie barely noticed it being done. The older paramedic checked her pupils while his partner placed two fingers on Clarissa's carotid artery to check her pulse. The younger of the two cleared airways and an oxygen mask was quickly placed over her mouth. "Does anyone know her name?" he looked up at the crowd.

"Clarissa. Clarissa Jones" said Janie in a shaky voice. The paramedic jotted it down too. "I need an address," he stated, "Does she have a purse?"

Janie turned to get it from the ground beside her. "Here." She could barely talk, her throat seemed to have closed over. She held her shaking hands tightly clasped. The young paramedic quickly found Clarissa's wallet with I.D. cards, and copied something down before placing the purse on a stretcher with Clarissa.

"Miss, are you a friend or family member?" The younger paramedic was speaking to her. "We need to get her to the hospital."

"No, no I just met her here a few days ago." Her voice shook. "Wait, where are you taking her?"

"Salt Lake City Regional Hospital Miss." He handed her a card with the hospital name, address and phone number. "You can call to see how she is." Janie thanked them.

"You bet." With that they were gone.

15

The crowd was whispering and buzzing. A police officer who had arrived at the scene encouraged everyone to leave the area and let traffic get moving again. Janie stood for a moment, stunned and unable to think clearly. She looked around but the man with the Mickey Mouse watch was nowhere in sight. She remembered Clarissa's briefcase and her notes. She had to get them and hold them until Clarissa returned. Janie looked around but could not spot the briefcase. Her own purse and bag were where she'd dropped them. She had carried most of Clarissa's belongings as well as her own but had Clarissa been carrying anything else? She closed her eyes and pictured them leaving the library. Clarissa had held on to her water bottle and purse but that was it. The purse had fallen to the pavement and was now with the Paramedics but the water bottle was nowhere in sight. Had it rolled away? Or been kicked away when the crowd gathered? That didn't explain the missing leather case full of Clarissa's research notes. Janie puzzled over it for a moment then a horrific thought came to her. Surely the leather briefcase hadn't been stolen by someone in the crowd? Who would do such a thing? While Clarissa lay in such critical condition would someone be crass enough to steal her expensive case?

Two concerned bystanders helped Janie pick up her own purse and bag but no one came forward with Clarissa's briefcase. She turned towards the police officer. Perhaps she should report the missing case. As she approached he waved her away. "Nothing more to see here Ma'am, please move along." With that he turned away to encourage other onlookers back to the sidewalk. Janie hesitated, then decided she'd report the missing case later.

Exhausted and red-faced from the heat, Janie slowly made her way back to the library. She needed a drink and wished she had found Clarissa's water bottle. Normally the last thing she'd do would be drink from someone else's bottle but she was overheated and thirsty. As much as she detested using public fountains, she stopped at the closest one once she reached the library. A long drink of refreshing cold water refreshed and cooled her off. Continuing to their readers she saw that Clarissa's carrel had her laptop still chained to the table, two empty boxes, two reels, a pen and a pencil.

She needed to retrieve Clarissa's laptop and check that nothing else had been left behind before phoning the hospital to check on Clarissa. She wasn't sure what to do about the laptop. Presumably the key was either in Clarissa's purse or the missing briefcase. She really didn't want to bother the attendants. If she could lift the carrel leg she could slip the cable out and take the laptop with her. Just to keep it safe until it could be returned to Clarissa. Bending down she saw that the cable was between the horizontal bar between the front legs and the underside of the carrel reading area. It would be impossible to get the laptop without cutting the cable. Sighing, she straightened and made her way to the attendant's window. They assured her that the custodian would cut the cable after closing, and the laptop would be held safely until Clarissa returned.

I better phone the hospital, she thought. Clarissa didn't look very good when they took her away. A phone call to the hospital resulted in her being transferred from one department to the next until finally someone asked her "Are you a friend or family member?" Knowing the hospital was unlikely to provide the information she wanted to someone who was only a friend, she lied. "I'm her sister."

"I'm sorry to inform you that your sister was dead on arrival. Would you care to come and claim her effects?"

Janie found herself holding her arms tightly across her chest. She felt numb but managed to end the conversation with the clerk. Death was not something new to her but Clarissa's death had shocked and shaken her deeply. Maybe she should go back to the hotel until she felt better. But she needed to collect her own things first. As she neared the carrels where she and Clarissa had been working just an hour before, she saw that one of Clarissa's microfilms was still on the reel.

Wondering what Clarissa had been looking at before she died, Janie sat and turned the reader lamp back on. A page from the New York Times dated July 10, 1880 met her intent gaze. Slowly she began to read through the articles and advertisements. Dozens of headlines filled the page: All Eyes on the Faster: The End Predicted to be Near at Hand; The Monmouth Park Races; Miscellaneous City News; Funeral of Col. W. T. Pelton; City & Suburban News: Brooklyn, New York, Westchester County, New Jersey; A Pauper at 2 Months Old; The Death of a Cousin of President Monroe in Paterson; New Sweepstakes at Saratoga; Charged With Murder; Tunneling the Hudson; Feeding the Immigrants; Suit Between Steamship Owners; A Corner & A Fight; Emmet the Actor; Educational Matters; The Concert at the Battery; Relieving Harlem's Sick Poor; The British-American Rifle Match; Passengers Arrived; Marine Intelligence.

She had no clue which article Clarissa had been interested in. What name or names had caught her attention? There were so many! A woman in Brooklyn committing suicide. A young boy arrested by police. An abandoned child found on a doorstep. A man charged with counterfeiting. A suit for slander. A grammar school teacher fined. Drowning death of a 13 year old boy. Arrests in New Jersey. A 7 year old boy run over by a cart. A woman dying after falling down a flight of stairs.

As curious as she was, Janie did not see how she could possibly figure out what Clarissa's cry of delight had been based on. But because it came just before her unfortunate death, Janie decided she would copy the page and tuck it away in her research bag in case she wanted to study it more at a later date.

Her thoughts drifted to Clarissa. She couldn't think, couldn't focus, couldn't comprehend how Clarissa could be dead when just a half hour before she'd been talking to her. It was time to leave but she wasn't sure she wanted to be alone at the hotel. She would call Steven and ask him to come back early.

16

Janie found a seat in the courtyard and with trembling hands, retrieved her cell phone and brought up Steven's number. Tears welled up in her eyes as she filled him in briefly and asked him to come back to Salt Lake. She was more shaken than she realized, and Steven agreed without hesitation. He'd be there as soon as possible. Hanging up, she closed her eyes and tried to regain her composure. She needed to sit for a bit longer.

"Ma'am? Ma'am excuse me, I don't mean to intrude." She looked up, squinting against the sun and saw a tall sturdily built man standing over her. His face was in shadow, and his entire body was backlit by the sun behind him. He moved slightly and she recognized the Native American looking man with the Mickey Mouse watch who had been on the street taking Clarissa's pulse.

"I saw your friend collapse earlier and I thought you'd want to know that someone took her leather case. I'm sure she'll be looking for it when she gets out of the hospital."

Janie was startled. "You saw someone steal her bag?"

He shook his head, his steely gray eyes staring intently at her. "No, I didn't see who took it but it's missing. I thought you'd want to know."

"And how do you know it's missing?" she was suspicious now. "Have you been following us?" Her voice had a ring of hostility tinged with apprehension.

"No, no. I'm only trying to help."

"Who are you?" Janie demanded. He hesitated, then answered, "I'm an ex-cop. It's my job to notice things and that's how I happened to see your friend's case go missing."

"Ex-cop? You look way too young to be retired." Janie's voice was full of suspicion.

He appeared taken aback. "Well, yeah I guess. I took early retirement."

Janie took her time while she stared at him. "Okay unless cop salaries have improved a whole lot, you're not living off your cop pension. You must be working at something else. So what is it –

Security Guard or P.I.?"

Hesitating briefly, he pulled out a business card. "I'm a Private Investigator."

Janie took the offered card and read his name - Daniel Mulroney, Private Investigator. His address and phone numbers were imprinted below. "So, why were you watching Clarissa?"

"I wasn't watching her. But it's hard to turn off years of training. I notice discrepancies and things that are out of place or suspicious."

"Then why are you at the library? I don't see any research notes." Janie's voice made it clear she wanted answers.

"It's nothing to do with your friend. Listen I was only trying to help. But there is one more thing." He hesitated. "Someone's been watching you. Or your friend, I'm not sure which. It's a guy, he's been walking around with a picture of a woman and checking you two out."

Janie was startled and it showed. "Tall, well dressed one day, then in scummy clothes the next?" she asked.

"Yeah that's the guy." He stared at her. "Do you know him?"

"No but I saw him too. It seemed a little off with his clothes and all. Who wears expensive stuff one day and dirty rags the next?"

"Yeah, well, I need to get going. I didn't mean to intrude, just felt I needed to let you know someone's watching you or your friend and that her case is gone." He turned to leave. Impulsively Janie said quietly, "She's dead."

He stopped and turned back to her. "Dead? Your friend?"

She nodded her head. "I just phoned the hospital and they said she was dead when she arrived." Now it was her turn to stare at him. She wasn't buying his story that it was all just a big coincidence that he happened to be in the library and he happened to notice Clarissa's case was missing and he happened to spot the guy with the picture in his hand.

His steely eyes had not even flickered. "Sorry for your loss then ma'am, and just keep in mind about that guy watching you." Giving her a little nod, he left, crossing the street at the lights for Temple Square. He soon disappeared through the gates. Probably taking a shortcut to one of the side streets, she thought.

Staring at the card he had given her she tried to think clearly. But her thoughts were jumbled, her mind leaping from one thing to the next. She realized she'd stayed in the courtyard longer than she'd intended and Steven might be at the hotel already. He'd be wondering where she was. As if on cue, her cell vibrated and as expected it was Steven. "Babe I'm back at the room, where the heck are you?"

"On my way, sorry. Don't worry, I'll be right there."

Once she was back in their room and being held by Steven, Janie found herself feeling somewhat calmer. She wasn't new to death but this one had shaken her. Moving apart, Janie sat on the green couch by the window while she filled him in on everything that had happened. As she spoke she voiced her misgivings and her feelings that something wasn't right. Steven sat across from her in an overstuffed armchair, leaning forward with his elbows on his knees. He listened intently, never once interrupting her. When she stopped, obviously done, he leaned back in the chair. "Hon, I understand why you're upset. But I think there are a whole lot of co-incidences here. You know you like to connect things that sometimes turn out to have nothing in common."

"I know that Steven. But she's dead. And someone was watching her. More than one someone actually, don't forget the weird little bird-like man I saw at the airport. And then there's her ex. He came in and almost assaulted her!"

"Almost being the operative word sweetheart. He was pissed. Ex husbands get that way sometimes. It doesn't mean he killed her. That's where you're going isn't it? You're determined to find a murder in all this." Steven stretched his long legs as he spoke.

"Why would anyone steal her briefcase? And her research notes? And what happened to her water bottle? It's all too much. One thing missing or out of place, okay maybe there's a simple explanation. But that's way too many for my liking."

Steven joined her on the couch. Taking her feet he placed them in his lap and began to rub them. "Sweetheart, don't start, okay? You're tired, in shock, someone you were getting to know just died suddenly. And now you're trying to connect dots that probably don't connect. Why don't you have a nap then let's go out for the rest of the day. Tomorrow you can go back to the library and get back into your own research on your great-whatever grandmother."

Janie wisely held her tongue. She knew when Steven was done listening. She'd take part of his advice – the part about having a nap. Tomorrow she'd start making a list of all the weird things that happened, maybe do some research into the stuff Clarissa was working on. Finding Clarissa's ex might not be a bad idea either. Maybe she'd even start on that list later today. She smiled at Steven as she told a small lie. "I think you're right about the nap sweetie, but after I wake up I'm going to head back to the library, get right back into my own research. Try to take my mind off what happened."

She wasn't sure she'd fooled Steven. He wasn't used to her acquiescing without a fight. He hesitated for one brief moment, then asked if she minded if he left for a bit, saying he might as well go on a walking tour of South State Street while she slept. Her mind was racing and she could hardly wait to get back to the library but she forced herself to lie still for several minutes after Steven donned his Fedora and left the room. She knew something was wrong and she was darned well going to figure it out.

17

Katie held back her long hair with one hand while she retched violently into the commode. Becky glanced at her as she dressed. "Goodness Katie, I wish you would make it to the water closet to do that!" She wrinkled her nose in disgust. "You've been sick every morning now for a week!"

Tightening the bodice of her housemaid dress and donning her freshly starched white apron, Becky gave Katie a knowing look. "Don't let the Missus catch you out Katie." With that Becky was gone, off to begin her morning chores in the kitchen.

Katie managed to stumble to her feet. She was exhausted and felt so ill. She had no idea what kind of grippe this was but it had hit her hard. If only Joey were here to talk to. But Joey left the city a year ago to find a job in Chicago. Neither one of them had a lot of schooling but they could write their names and a simple note but she hadn't had a letter from him in months.

She dressed as quickly as she could, feeling another wave of nausea coming on. She sat on the double bed that she and Becky shared and pulled her lisle stockings on. After finally managing to get the stockings on straight, she tugged her chemise over her head. Then she worked her arms into her shirt, tugging at the front as she forced the buttons through their holes. Lord she was gaining weight. Her shirt was tight across her bosom! She felt as if she was bursting out of her chemise but she managed to button the shirt and put on her crisply starched apron. Winded from the exertion she stood to pull on her full gray skirt. A wave of dizziness struck and she was forced to sit down until it passed. Tucking up her long hair and pinning it in place, she sat her starched white housemaid's cap on top. That will do, she thought as she caught a glimpse of herself in the little mirror atop the one dresser in the room. She had to hurry. Mrs. Teadley could be such a tyrant if the girls were late in the morning.

Last week while she was scouring the pots in the hot soapy water, she felt quite faint and had to lean against the big counter for a moment. Mrs. Teadley, who was in charge of the younger girls, was furious and scolded Katie for several minutes. She did not dare provoke that wrath again!

Hurrying down the backstairs, Katie realized she'd forgotten to rinse her mouth and the taste of bile was bringing on another bout of nausea. She rushed through the back kitchen door to be met with Mrs. Teadley's disapproving stare. Hastily Katie began breaking open eggs from the large bowl on the butcher block counter. Every morning she cracked six eggs for Mrs. Teadley to prepare breakfast for the Master and Missus. This morning the sight of the yellow yolk quivering in the runny whites of the eggs caused a huge wave of revolt in her stomach. Clutching her mouth with her hands, she ran to the sink where she promptly retched. Mrs. Teadley shrieked and the kitchen girls turned to stare, mouths agape.

"You! Girl! What are you doing?" Mrs. Teadley's voice rose to glass-breaking pitch.

"Sorry, please excuse me ma'am," Katie mumbled as she wiped her mouth with her apron, "I'm not feeling well."

Becky snickered in the corner and winked at Annie, another kitchen maid. "Oh yes, a bit of fun she had and now she's got to pay the piper!" The girls snickered until Mrs. Teadley turned a stern eye on them. "Enough," she warned. "Girl, I will speak to you immediately after breakfast is served to Sir and Missus. Now get yourself back to work and do not make such a commotion in my kitchen again!"

Katie's face, always pale, turned even whiter as she thought about what Becky had said. Could it be? Was it possible? She was an innocent when they had lain together the first time and in all the times since she'd not dared to ask about such matters. Her ma had no children after Katie so she didn't know much about being with child, but she remembered a neighbor woman talking about how violently ill she was. Come to think of it, her monthly times seemed overdue.

In an agony of dread, Katie managed to finish her morning chores. She was terrified that Mrs. Teadley would report her to the Missus and she'd be sacked from her position. Then what would she do? With Joey gone and no lodgings of her own, she'd be out on the street. She shivered with apprehension but reminded herself *that her lover would surely look after her. After all, he'd told her she was beautiful, given her a small gold locket with her name engraved on it, and hinted that they might one day be together. She knew he was married and it was wrong but she went to church every Sunday and confessed her sins to Father Mulroney. She'd said enough Hail Marys in the last month to last a lifetime!*

18

Janie awoke with a start and sat up to check the clock on the bedside table. She hadn't meant to fall asleep but luckily it was one of her five minute power naps. Steven was still out so she could start making notes about Clarissa's death. She planned to jot down every suspicious or off-kilter thing she'd seen in the past three days, then take a good look at her notes and try to figure out what was going on. You never knew when something would be the clue needed to solve a puzzle.

She needed to create a flow chart, the same kind she made in her genealogy research. She needed to make a list of the people she thought might have had something to do with Clarissa's death. Lists were her thing. Steven and her son both teased her about her never-ending lists scribbled on the backs of envelopes, bills, receipts, even tissue boxes. But lists helped her organize her thoughts and as much as she loved technology, she was old school when it came to certain things like lists. And a list was definitely needed now.

Because the more she thought about it the more convinced she was that Clarissa's death was not what it seemed. After making her flow chart, she had descriptions of four people whose behavior had struck her as odd. Birdman, as she had begun to call him – the little man all in black who she'd first seen at the airport. Clarissa's ex or soon-to-be ex-husband. The man roaming around the library checking faces against a photo while leaving a trail of expensive cologne in his wake, and last but not least, the private investigator who had spoken to her after Clarissa's sudden death.

She also wrote down several puzzling events. No matter what Steven said or thought, she was going to see what she could find out about each person and event on her list. The ex-husband seemed as good a place to start as any, and she had a strong feeling he was involved. She remembered that when he came in and accosted Clarissa he'd been wearing a green polo shirt that had the name of a landscaping company across the back. Clarissa had mentioned that he owned his own business and she'd called

62

him Ken. Janie needed a phone book. Time to check landscaping businesses in Salt Lake even if she had to phone each one to ask if Ken Jones was the owner. She hoped she had time to do that before Steven returned. The last thing she wanted was for him to see her embroiled in another mysterious death.

She ran her finger down the list. Jones Landscaping Services was listed partway down the page. An address and phone number were on the next line. *No time like the present,* she thought and before she could chicken out, she dialed the number. After two rings a cheerful voice answered. "Jones Landscaping, this is Linda."

After giving an automatic response, Janie asked if Ken Jones was in. Her heartbeat quickened at the receptionist's answer. "No he's not. May I take a message? I'm afraid he's not available at the moment."

Janie assured the receptionist that no message was required and she would call back. She hung up before the woman could protest. A look of determination came over her face. Steven called it her "Uh-oh, look out, Janie's on a mission!" expression. Quickly scribbling down the address of Jones Landscaping, she grabbed her sweater and purse and hurried out of the room. She would text Steven on the way and make some excuse for her absence.

19

As the driver made his way to the address she gave him, Janie took the opportunity to go over what she planned to say and do. Soon she was standing outside the doors of Jones Landscaping. A deep breath to steady her nerves and she was inside. A bottle blonde woman in her late 30s sat at a gray metal desk. The smell of nail polish filled the air and Janie realized the woman was painting her long nails in a bubble gum pink color. As Janie drew closer to the desk she saw the nameplate on her desk that read Linda Thompson. Pausing in the middle of a swipe with the nail polish applicator, the receptionist looked up. "Hello, can I help you?"

Janie put all her acting abilities into effect. "Yes, thank you. I'm looking for Ken. I'm a friend of his wife." The receptionist's eyes flickered. Her face crumbled slightly. "Oh. Oh dear, well ummm Ken's not here right now. You say you're a friend of Clarissa's?"

"Yes that's right. I'm just in town for the day and I wanted to say hi to Clarissa but I've misplaced her phone number. So I thought of Ken."

"Oh dear, then you don't know." Linda's face crumbled even more. "Oh my, I am so sorry to be the one to tell you but Clarissa passed away this morning."

Janie feigned shock. Her hand flew to her chest, her eyes widened. "What? No, that can't be! I just spoke to her last week! When did she die? How? I can't believe it. No!" She forced moisture to well up in her eyes, then pulling out a crumpled tissue from her purse, dabbed daintily at the corners. In a soft voice she asked, "Do you have a glass of water? Could I sit down? Oh I feel so shaky. This is so upsetting."

Linda's face took on a concerned look. "Yes of course, here, sit down in my chair while I get you some water."

"No, no I don't want to inconvenience you. Do you think I could wait for Ken in his office?" She forced her voice to quiver and a few tears rolled down her cheeks.

"Of course, this way." She led Janie to an office with a closed door, opened it and showed her inside. "He should be back in an hour, are you okay waiting in here?"

Janie smiled sweetly and reassured the woman that she would be fine, she just needed time to compose herself before Ken returned. She dabbed again at her eyes with her tissue. "Water would be lovely dear," she said, and the receptionist left, returning in a minute with a glass of tepid water. "Thank you dear, I'll just sit here and wait." Her eyes took in a small windowless office not much bigger than a closet. It looked and smelled like it hadn't been cleaned in a very long time.

She sat in a hard wooden chair that faced an old beat up metal desk overflowing with papers. On the other side was an office chair on wheels, its once new leather now marred with scratches and nicks, its color a faded black. Three tall metal filing cabinets took up one wall with stacks of paper towering almost to the ceiling. Cardboard boxes were shoved haphazardly into a corner, leaving just enough room for a row of four 2-drawer filing cabinets on top of which sat a coffee pot, a photocopier, and a fax machine.

Several half full mugs of coffee sat on various surfaces. All of them had that slick oily film on top as if they'd sat there for days. The dented metal wastebasket beside the desk was overflowing with empty Starbucks cups. In front of her was a scattered pile of half-eaten sunflower seeds. The overpowering smell of stale cigar smoke filled Janie's nostrils and she wrinkled her nose in disgust. An overflowing ashtray perched near the edge of the metal desk gave testimony to Ken's addiction.

With Linda gone, Janie got up and quietly closed the office door. Her heart was beating so fast it felt like it might jump out of her chest. This was her chance. She planned on going through his desk drawers, his filing cabinets, his Rolodex, anything she had time to go through before he showed up. She wasn't sure what she was looking for but she'd know it if she found it.

The middle desk drawer was locked but the top one on the right opened with ease. Inside was a jumble of pens, paperclips, elastic bands, nail clippers, nail file and other miscellaneous items. Nothing that was of interest to Janie. The bottom drawer, much deeper, held a bottle of Tums, a box of cigars, a bottle of Bourbon, and two greasy glasses. She turned her attention to the desktop. A computer that looked like it had seen better days sat on the right. A rolodex bursting at the seams sat to the left along with a phone with several phone lines, most of them blinking red. Since Ken's landscaping business didn't appear to be a hive of activity, Janie assumed that the receptionist had put all the lines on hold while she did her nails.

An old fashioned blotter stained with years of coffee spills lay in the middle. Tucked into the corners was an assortment of papers. It looked like bills or invoices and Janie quickly began rifling through them. She stopped at an invoice for various pesticides. Scribbled on it was the notation *extremely toxic*. A flyer for what looked like a weedkiller was tucked under the invoice and on it was the scribbled notation, *fatal if swallowed*. Rummaging in her purse, she pulled out her phone and began snapping pictures. She didn't have time to write down the long names of the chemicals and insecticides he seemed interested in but she could take photos to look at later on her laptop. Click. Click. She snapped a few pictures of some of the papers on the desk and filing cabinets while she was at it.

She kept glancing at the door and listening for the sounds of Ken returning. Nothing yet. Her attention turned to his rolodex. She flipped the cards at random, eyes alert, yet not knowing why she was bothering. How would she even know if she found a name that was important? She stopped flipping cards. Turned back one that she'd just turned over. The name Dan Mulroney leaped out at her. His business card was stapled to a rolodex index card. Why would Ken have the phone number of Private Investigator Daniel Mulroney, the man who had approached her in the courtyard of the library?

Ken's clunker of a computer was powered up so Janie took a quick breath and tapped the keyboard. She was going for his email. There might be something revealing there. People didn't usually protect their email accounts very well and chances were that he used the one that came with his ISP. If so, there was a good chance he had it set for an automatic login, so there might be no need for his password and username. If not, she could check for a freemail account. His username and password would probably be written somewhere – either on a rolodex card or on a piece of paper tucked under his blotter. She lifted the stained blotter and smiled. There it was, scribbled on a piece of paper.

sonejk@freemail.com
password loverboynumber1

Cute, she thought. *Someone's got a big ego.* His browser opened at Google's homepage so all she had to do was type in freemail and then log into his account once the new page loaded. There. She was in. Emails from dan@mulroney.com flashed on the screen. Opening the most recent she saw what looked like a report labeled CJones1.6.09 attached as a doc file. She didn't think she had time to open it but read the covering email. Rapidly skimming the email she saw that it was from Daniel to Ken and that he was bringing Ken up to date on what he'd found that week. Not much help except that now she knew Ken had hired a private investigator to watch Clarissa. Or had he been hired to kill her?

20

Time was growing short. She'd been in Ken's office at least forty-five minutes. No time to waste, so as much as she wanted to read the doc file she ignored it and looked for other emails that might be of interest. She was annoyed at herself for not bringing her flash drive, she could have downloaded that doc file in seconds and read it later in her hotel room. However she could forward the email to her personal account, erase the copy in his SENT mail folder, and hope that he wasn't computer savvy enough to figure out what had happened. The slight danger was that the next time he manually typed in someone's email address, if it started with the same letters as her account, her name would pop up. However her email address only contained her first name so even if he realized it was her, he had no way of tracking her down. And she wanted that file. After a few seconds of hesitation she decided not to forward the email. She didn't feel comfortable taking that chance and possibly arousing Ken's suspicions.

Emails from Clarissa came into view, as well as replies from Ken. The most recent from Ken to Clarissa was shocking in its hostility.

You bitch, do you think you can get away with this?
Don't push me too hard or you'll be sorry.

Janie heard noises out front and not wanting to take any chances on being discovered snooping, she quickly closed the browser window and sat down. Closing her eyes, she willed her breathing to deepen and her heart to slow down. The office door was thrust open and in strode the man she recognized as Clarissa's ex-husband. Placing a hand on her chest she stood up slowly and said, "Oh you must be Ken. I'm Janie, Clarissa's friend. I'm so sorry to hear about her passing." Another swipe at the corner of her eyes to convince him. He said nothing, simply stood there staring. She offered a hand, and he begrudgingly gave it a brief handshake. He perched on the corner of his desk.

"Clarissa's friend? I don't remember her mentioning anyone called Janie."

"Yes, we met online, we've been chatting back and forth in

email for a few years now. I'm in town for a few days and we were supposed to get together. She mentioned in her last email that she was going to be here researching." It was hard to do but once more Janie managed a bit of moisture in her eyes. "And now I've just learned of her death."

"Yeah that's right she dropped dead a few hours ago so it looks like you just missed her."

Janie hesitated before asking "Was she ill? I had no idea she was sick."

Ken walked around his desk, stooped and opened the bottom drawer. Taking the box of cigars out, he placed it on the desk, opened it and chose one carefully. Rolling it in his fingers, he seemed lost in thought as he sat down.

"Yeah she was complaining of chest pains and headaches for awhile. I told her she should see a doctor but you know Clarissa. Stubborn as a mule." He kept his gaze on Janie's face. "So tell me more about how you met Clarissa."

"Well we hadn't met in person, just online. Through APG."

He looked puzzled.

"Association of Professional Genealogists" She took a chance, figuring the lie would hold up. "We both belong and that's how we met."

"Oh, yeah that stuff," came the response. "So what can I do for you? Why'd you hang around to see me?"

"I just wanted to express my condolences and ask when the funeral will be. And where."

"Geez I dunno, it's not my concern." Ken gave a dismissive wave of his arm. "Me and Clarissa were in the middle of a divorce, so I dunno what's gonna happen to her now."

"You don't seem concerned either." Janie responded. His eyes narrowed and he leaned forward, his chair creaking as he did so. With a menacing look he spoke "And what's it to you? You got a problem? Take it somewhere else lady."

Janie knew it was time to leave so she stood up and quietly said, "Thank you for your time and once again, my condolences on your loss." He made no move to see her to the door, instead he sat without saying a word as she let herself out. At the receptionist desk she asked Linda to phone a taxi. "Where are you going?" Linda asked. "They'll want to know." Janie saw that Ken was now standing in his office doorway listening to their exchange. "Little America Hotel," Janie lied. No way was she going to let Ken know where she was really staying. Once she was safely in the cab she'd just tell the driver she'd changed her mind. The taxi couldn't come soon enough to suit her but she knew it might take 20 minutes or more. She smiled at Linda and told her she'd wait outside in the fresh air. She felt Ken's eyes on her back watching every step she took as she left the building. By the time she reached the sidewalk her head was pounding with the start of a tension headache. Thank goodness Steven didn't know what she was up to. He'd be furious.

21

On the taxi ride back to her hotel she thought over what she'd found in Ken's office, and what Ken had said. She knew he'd lied about Clarissa complaining of chest pains and headaches. She'd told Janie she rarely got headaches. Besides, his body language and face had indicated he was lying. She'd watched him closely as he spoke and when his eyes suddenly shifted to the right, she knew it was a lie. And Clarissa had told Janie that she and her ex were barely on speaking terms. No way would she ever have shared her ailments with him. Janie was still mulling over the conversation in his office when the taxi pulled into the semi-circular drive of the hotel.

She checked the time when she was back in her room. She was eager to transfer the photos from her phone to her laptop but she might not be able to do it before Steven came back. He'd have a fit if he found out what she'd done. Better to wait until she was at the library. But there was still some time before Steven returned. Something had occurred to her on the ride over. Clarissa's purse was at the hospital where she'd been taken. And in that purse was her cell phone. If Janie could get the purse she could access the phone and see all the outgoing calls Clarissa had made. Incoming calls would show too. She could find out who Clarissa called that morning in the library. She definitely wanted to know about the call that left Clarissa excited.

Scribbling a hasty note for Steven, saying she was going to a second-hand bookstore, she gulped two headache pills then dashed out of the room, praying that a taxi would be waiting out front. She was in luck. It didn't take long to get to the hospital but she had to listen to her driver talking non-stop about the city, his family and his dog. At least when she asked if he would wait for her, he agreed. Moving quickly up the sidewalk and through the massive front doors, she headed for the admissions desk. The antiseptic hospital smells were not as strong as she'd expected but they still assaulted her sensitive nostrils. She told the clerk in Admissions the story she'd rehearsed in the cab on the ride over; that she was Clarissa Jones' sister and wanted to pick up her sister's purse.

For the next twenty minutes she was directed from one person to the next until finally a young woman checked her computer and said "Clarissa Jones. Yes we had her purse and some jewelry she was wearing when she was brought here, but everything has been claimed."

"Claimed?" Janie could not hide the surprise in her voice. "I don't understand. Who claimed it?"

The woman tipped her head back to see her monitor better. "Let's see, it says here that her brother claimed her effects."

Janie's mind raced. Her brother! Clarissa had told her that she was an only child. Someone had posed as her brother and come to the hospital to get her things. The woman at the desk was looking at Janie expectantly. Janie thought quickly. "Oh my brothers, for goodness sake you'd think they could have told me and saved me a trip. Can you tell me which one picked up my sister's things?"

"Let me see, it says Harold."

Not much help there, thought Janie. But I guess I couldn't really expect someone to leave their real name. "Oh, Harold. Did he leave an address by any chance?"

The young woman's brows wrinkled. "You need your brother's address?" she asked in a puzzled tone.

Janie was floundering and couldn't think of any way to explain why she would need her brother's address. "Oh no, of course not. Forgive me, I'm still in shock over my sister's death. It's been a terrible few days and I'm not thinking clearly. Thank you so much for your help." With that she turned to go. "You bet," came the woman's response as she swiveled her chair around to answer a ringing phone.

Her taxi was still waiting as promised and Janie climbed in. She sat back and began thinking about this new development. Someone wanted Clarissa's purse badly enough to go to the hospital and lie to get it. Add that to the missing briefcase and it looked like someone was covering their tracks. And if that were the case it meant her hunch was right and Clarissa's death was not what it seemed. Murder. Clarissa had been murdered. There was no other explanation.

As her taxi pulled out of the hospital parking lot, Janie noticed a familiar figure further down the sidewalk. It was Dan Mulroney, the Private Detective who'd approached her at the library right after Clarissa collapsed. Puzzled, she frowned. Her throbbing head made it difficult to think straight. But her suspicions were aroused by seeing him there.

Janie arrived at the hotel hoping that Steven had not yet returned. She didn't like keeping things from him and she especially hated telling him lies, even though she considered them little white lies that didn't hurt anyone. Still, they were lies. And that didn't sit well with her. Much to her chagrin Steven was already in their room, stretched out on the king size bed watching yet another re-run of Star Trek. He loved that show and could watch any episode dozens of times without tiring of it. She was sure he'd seen them all a hundred times.

They exchanged hellos and questions about their respective days but when Steven asked her what good books she'd found at the bookstore, Janie fended off his question. "Oh look at the time. Hon, I'm gonna grab a quick shower and then we can go for dinner, okay?"

Forty-five minutes later they were on their way to Market Street Grill. Janie needed to relax. She was determined not to share her thoughts with Steven because that would mean revealing everything she'd been up to. She knew him well enough to know he would not be pleased. But she did need to plan tomorrow's day and figure out what her next step would be.

Sunlight was peeking around the edges of the hotel room drapes. Janie opened her eyes, stretched, and thought about getting up. Steven was already out of bed which was unusual. She blinked, rubbed her eyes and tried to focus on the clock radio beside her. 7:47 a.m. She'd slept in this morning. And Steven was up early, she could hear water running in the bathroom. She sniffed the air. Was that coffee she smelled?

"Good morning sweetheart." Steven's cheerful voice greeted her. "You're a sleepyhead today." His smiling face peered down at her. "I put coffee on for you. Are you ready for a cup?"

Janie couldn't function without her two cups of coffee first thing in the morning. What a nice treat to have Steven make some and bring it to her in bed. Sitting up against the pillows she took her first sip, eyes closed. *Ambrosia*, she thought. *Nectar of the Gods.*

"Sweetie, I'm gonna head out early today if you don't mind. I thought I'd go back to the Airplane Museum, then if there's time I'd like to take a drive out to the Salt Lake, spend some time on Antelope Island. If you'd like to go with me I could come back and get you." Steven sat on the edge of the bed as he told her his plans for the day.

"I'd rather keep working at the library if you're okay with that." She touched his hand and his fingers curled gently around hers. He leaned over, kissed the top of her head and said, "How long have I been married to you? I know what you love to do, it's no problem. We'll catch up at supper time, okay? I'll call you later and see how you're doing."

"Do you want to have breakfast downstairs before you go?" Janie asked. Secretly she hoped not but if he wanted her to join him, she'd get up and get ready.

"Nah, that's okay, you look too comfortable where you are. I'll stop along the way to the Museum. Why don't you treat yourself to room service this morning?"

"Mmmm. Good idea." Janie snuggled down a bit more under the covers, coffee cup still in hand. Steven laughed. "Doesn't take much to please you, does it?" Janie smiled up at him. She had a big day planned and was anxious for him to leave. She felt a twinge of guilt but told herself it wasn't really a big deal, it wasn't that she didn't enjoy his company, she just had other things on her mind.

"Okay babe, I'm outta here, talk atcha' later!" They shared a brief been-married-forever kiss on the lips, and with a wave he was gone. Janie gulped the rest of her coffee then phoned room service. She figured she had lots of time to shower and dress before it arrived.

About thirty minutes later her order of eggs over easy, wheat toast no butter, hash browns, and one blueberry pancake on the side arrived. A steaming carafe of coffee completed the breakfast. She tipped the server, signed for the food then sat at the desk and pulled out her laptop. The first thing she wanted to do was check out the pictures she took in Ken Jones' office.

Transferring the photos from her phone to her hard drive she opened her graphic program and enlarged each one, studying them carefully. The flyer on herbicides and insecticides was in focus and easy to read. Connecting to the internet via the hotel's WiFi she was able to search the names of the various drugs. She followed that task by researching the invoice for insecticides on Ken's desk. Thanks to her pictures she could look up all of them.

After more than an hour of reading about pesticides, insecticides, herbicides and other chemicals used in landscaping, her head was spinning. Much of what she found was incomprehensible to her, being so scientific as to be over her head. But it seemed that diquat and paraquat, two of the pesticides she'd found listed in Ken's paperwork were highly toxic and were known to have caused deaths. In fact paraquat was often the suicide poison of choice. That shocked her. *Imagine swallowing such a horrible poison!* She shuddered at the thought.

Other pesticides, herbicides and insecticides were also considered harmful but she had trouble understanding what dosage might be needed to kill a human and how it could be administered. But she'd noted the names on Ken's papers, mainly rotenone, nicotine and something with the active ingredient imidacloprid. Some websites stated that many pesticides were toxic if an asthma sufferer inhaled them. Many had accumulative effects when ingested or inhaled and it could take 48 hours to 10 days to kill.

She read that rotenone poisoning involved convulsions and cardiorespiratory arrest. A person could be poisoned by ingestion or inhalation. That fit Clarissa's symptoms but Janie had trouble finding out how much was needed to be considered a lethal dose. And how would Ken have administered it? Through food or drink most likely, but how? And when? Diquat and paraquat also piqued her interest. One study showed that diquat and paraquat had life threatening effects on the human GI tract, kidney, liver, heart and other organs. In case of paraquat poisoning, pulmonary fibrosis was the cause of death, while diquat affected the nervous system.

She continued reading. Ingestion of paraquat or diquat resulted in symptoms of burning pain in the mouth, throat, chest, and upper abdomen; pulmonary edema, pancreatic and other renal effects. Diarrhea could occur and it was often sometimes bloody. Giddiness, headache, fever, and coma often resulted from ingestion. If swallowed, the person could develop a nosebleed, vomit or have a seizure. Clarissa had a nosebleed and when she collapsed it looked like a seizure. Janie also remembered that Clarissa kept saying her throat hurt and that she kept taking swigs from her water bottle. And one more thing – she'd been choking and unable to breathe properly. That fit the symptoms of pulmonary edema she read about. She was pretty sure that meant some type of swelling of the lungs or lung tissue.

Death could occur almost immediately after paraquat was swallowed or it could take longer for symptoms to show. Diquat was a nervous system toxin and symptoms included nervousness, forgetfulness, unable to recognize people and so on. That didn't fit with Clarissa's symptoms but paraquat might just fit perfectly. The bottom line was that Ken had knowledge of, and ability to acquire, any number of poisons that could have killed Clarissa.

24

It was a warm day but clouds that were rolling in partially obscured the sun that she'd seen when she first woke up. She loved seeing the impressive library building in daylight. It seemed to soar overhead, all sharp lines and angles reaching up to the sky, an imposing monument. Striding quickly through the double doors of the library entrance, she was greeted pleasantly by a library volunteer. Nodding her head and returning his cheery good morning, she continued to the elevators and pressed the 2nd floor button. On the ride up it suddenly occurred to her that she had Ken Jones' passwords. She'd taken a photo of the page that contained dozens of passwords including his freemail account. That meant she could log in from her computer and access his mail any time she wanted. *What a chowderhead I can be*, she thought.

The reader she'd used the previous day was taken but she found another nearby. Janie disliked change and was grateful she was at least in the same row. She settled in and powered up her laptop. The battery was almost fully charged so she had a few hours to work from it. Within a few seconds she was at the freemail page on her browser, and logged into Ken's email. Now she could read the file that Daniel Mulroney had sent a few days ago.

She clicked to download the file CJones16.7.09.doc. After saving it to her hard drive she opened it in her editor and began to read. It was dated July 16 and addressed to Ken. Janie skimmed it fairly quickly but saw nothing of any interest other than the fact that it was a report of Clarissa's comings and goings from July 14 to 16. Nothing jumped out at her, it was rather boring, containing such items as "8:47 a.m. Subject left coffee shop and headed north on N. West Temple Street" "9:08 a.m. Subject arrived Family History Library, went to 2nd floor" Closing the file, Janie thought about what she'd read. The emails proved that Ken Jones, Clarissa's ex-husband, had hired Daniel Mulroney to follow Clarissa. But it didn't help Janie figure out why and how Clarissa died, or who killed her. Mind you, her money was still on the ex-husband or the private investigator.

The rustling of papers disturbed her and at almost the same moment her chair was bumped from behind. It wasn't unusual to be jostled as the aisles were narrow and people often forgot to push their chairs in when they left their readers. But Janie had pulled her chair in until it was touching the reader desk, so there should be lots of room for other patrons to get by. Turning, she saw that whoever sat at the reader behind her had left his chair about 10 inches away from hers. It was impossible for other researchers to make their way between the two chairs without bumping into her. Not wanting to be disturbed again, she stood to push in her chair.

That was when she saw him. The man who looked scummy but wore good quality cologne and a mega-expensive watch, was standing about thirty feet away. Even though it was dark in the microfilm reader area, it seemed like he was looking right at her. He wasn't holding anything this time and he didn't flinch from her stare. Heart pounding, she turned, fumbled for her purse and made a beeline for the attendant's window. *Let's see if he follows me* she thought.

Once at the window, she asked an innocuous question of the friendly volunteer behind the counter. Casually she risked a glance to her right, towards the microfilm reader area. Nothing. No one in bum's clothing was watching her or walking around. Thanking the attendant, she walked slowly to the bathrooms, trying to take in the room with sideways glances. No one that looked like him at the computers as far as she could see. Maybe she was over-reacting. Maybe Steven was right about her overactive imagination.

25

A few minutes in the bathroom fluffing her hair, and a quick drink at the water fountain all helped to calm her nerves. She decided to take the long route back to her carrel to see if she could spot him. By the time she sat down again she'd decided she was letting her imagination get the better of her. Reaching to open her laptop she paused, her hand suspended a few inches from the case. It was already open. The screensaver was flashing. But she'd closed it before grabbing her purse. It was an automatic ritual with her, she never left her laptop open when it was unattended. Steven joked that it was part of her obsessive-compulsive nature. So her laptop should not be sitting open in her carrel. She thought it might be slightly out of position too. The angle wasn't quite right for her to read it when she was seated. She'd never have used it in this position.

The file she'd been looking at was still open, so if someone had opened her laptop to see what she was doing, they'd have seen the Detective's report to Ken. But who would have that much nerve? And who would want to see what she was up to? Ken was one of several who came to mind, but she hadn't seen him in the library. Of course he could be in another row. She might not have noticed in the dim lighting.

Fishing in her purse, she pulled out her phone and quickly scrolled through for Ken's office number. A few rings later, a cheerful Linda answered and informed Janie he was out with a customer and did she want to leave a message. Janie hung up after reassuring Linda it wasn't important, she'd call back. That answered one question. Ken wasn't in his office and that meant he could be here in the building. Did she dare get up and walk up and down the reader aisles? Good grief, what if he'd looked at her laptop and knew she had access to his email? *Calm down*, she told herself sternly. *This is not the time to fall apart.* Her mind whirled. She needed to smarten up and go on full alert. She'd been in danger before and always come out unscathed. This time was no different. She just had to get into the zone and not take chances.

Taking a deep breath, she closed the open file and scrolled through Ken's emails. She wanted to read any exchanges he'd had with Clarissa or Dan the detective. She read through several until finding one that stood out. It was an email from Ken to Clarissa dated two days before Clarissa died. Ken asked her to meet him at a restaurant for lunch, saying he needed to talk to her and it was important. Clarissa had sent a brief reply agreeing to meet. Janie's mind was flipping through her memory banks. Wasn't there something about one of the pesticides Ken had shown interest in? Something about it taking forty-eight hours for death to occur? She checked her notes. There it was. Paraquat could take forty-eight hours or longer to kill. Ken could have slipped some into Clarissa's food or drink while they were at the restaurant. That would explain his not being seen at the library the morning of Clarissa's death. He had already poisoned her and therefore had no need to be in the vicinity.

Janie decided to finish checking Ken's emails then she'd take a break and sit and think about what she'd found. And what she needed to do next. An email from Dan Mulroney came into view. It was dated a week ago and confirmed the job for which he'd been hired, the surveillance of Clarissa, no firm end date for job completion, he was to track her movements and make notes on anyone she met. Also determine what bank accounts and safety deposit boxes she had. His hourly fee was agreed on. Basically it seemed to be a confirmation of an earlier phone conversation with Ken. Janie thought for a few moments then logged out of Ken's email account. She powered down her laptop, hesitated about leaving it during her break and decided it was going with her.

Seated outside in the courtyard with a turkey on wheat sandwich and bottle of water, Janie closed her eyes and tried to think things through. It was a bit cooler today so not as crowded outside and she didn't have the cacophony of voices and noise from other researchers to distract her. Nibbling on her sandwich, she realized she'd overlooked something important. What happened to Clarissa's body? Was she at the hospital? The coroner's office? Clarissa didn't have children and she was an only child. Who would bury her? Janie added finding out where

Clarissa's body was to her mental checklist of things to do.

One other thing to check on and that was the list of passwords from Ken's desk. It was a fairly long list and Janie hadn't had a good look at it yet. Her laptop still had some battery life so she unzipped her case and wrangled it out. Opening her graphic program she zoomed in on the text in the photo. Many of the usernames and passwords were for unknown places but Ken had a habit of putting abbreviations beside them which represented the specific site. *Jackpot* she thought. The third password down was labeled "bank". If she could figure out what bank he used, she could check his bank accounts, see if there were any suspicious transactions in the last month or so. She used Google to type in the text *Salt Lake City banks.*

A list of five banks popped up. They were Wells Fargo, Key, Zion, Liberty and CIT. She'd try them all until she got in with Ken's login and password. There might be more because she wasn't familiar with banks in the city but she might as well try those five first. Fifteen minutes later Janie was studying a list of Ken's deposits, withdrawals, and bill payments. For a brief moment she felt this level of spying on her part was wrong. And possibly illegal. But she reminded herself that she was trying to solve Clarissa's death and that there was an extremely good possibility that the ex-husband, Ken, had killed her. And there, staring her in the face, was a large withdrawal of $15,000.00 made in the week before Clarissa died. That was a pretty big sum of cash to be walking around with, Janie thought. Why wouldn't he write a check if he was paying a bill or buying something? Or put it on his credit card? Maybe it was time to go to the police with her suspicions. No, that wouldn't do, how would she explain knowing that he'd made a large cash withdrawal. She needed to think carefully about each step she should make now.

There didn't seem to be anything else of interest in Ken's account, so she logged out and closed her browser window. She sat very still with her laptop on her knees. She became aware of the chirping of the traffic lights. Funny how you could tune things out when you were focused on something else, but the minute you relaxed, the world rushed back at you. The vibration of her cell stopped her philosophical musings. It was Steven calling to tell her he planned on going to an Art Gallery showing tonight at 8 o'clock. He hoped they could go together after supper but she begged off. She didn't feel like standing around and discussing art and she knew Steven didn't mind going places alone. They agreed to meet for a quick bite at 6:30 at a nearby restaurant, and said their goodbyes. Janie smiled as she tucked her phone back into her purse. She really was lucky to have such a terrific husband. He never tried to make her do things she didn't want to do.

With her phone safely zipped back into its pocket, she brushed her hair out of her eyes and looked up. She was startled to see Birdman, as she thought of him, standing near her. His mouth was open as if he was about to speak. He stared at her for a brief moment but when he realized she was looking at him, his eyes began to shift sideways, rapidly moving from left to right and back again. He wore the same dark baggy jeans and grungy t-shirt with his long black trench coat. His thin greasy hair hung limply past his ears and beads of sweat dotted his forehead. *Who wears a trench coat in such hot weather*, she thought. He turned his head away from her stare, gave Janie a sideways glance, and took a hesitant step in her direction. Janie wondered if he were coming over to speak to her. His Adam's apple bobbed in his neck as he swallowed. Another step in her direction. His egg-shaped head began to bob up and down in rapid bird-like movements and he swallowed again, his mouth moving but no sound coming out. Janie was startled but decided to sit very still. She was afraid that any movement on her part would send him scurrying away. His odd behavior was disconcerting but she needed to find out what he wanted and if he was following her.

A young couple, arms around each other's waists, walked across the courtyard laughing loudly. They stumbled as they walked, then laughed at their clumsiness.

Hearing their laughter, Birdman swiveled his head further to the right, let out a tiny squawk and darted away. Once again his long skinny arms flapped as he rushed across the street in front of Temple Square.

26

Finding someone in the hospital who could tell her what happened to Clarissa's body took Janie over half an hour. She thought phoning would be the fastest way but was regretting that decision every time she told her story and was transferred to yet another department. "Hello, I'm Clarissa Jones' sister. She passed away yesterday in your hospital and I'm calling to find out where her remains are."

Finally a clipped female voice informed her, "Ms. Jones' remains were claimed by her brother."

"Our brother? Where did he take Clarissa?" Janie had to remember that she was pretending to be Clarissa's sister.

A brief pause. "I'm sure your brother could tell you."

"My brother and I haven't spoken in years," responded Janie. "I'd really appreciate it if you could tell me where he took her. I've just flown in from Canada and I don't want to miss her funeral service." She tried to put a quaver in her voice.

The clerk relented. "Yes, of course, let me just check my records." A brief moment later she was back. "Ms. Jones was picked up by Simpson Brothers Crematory this morning."

Cremation! Janie's thoughts were running wildly. Cremation meant there'd be no evidence of poisoning, no possible way to prove Clarissa had been murdered. The clerk was speaking. "Ma'am are you still there?"

"Yes, yes I am. Please forgive me, I'm feeling a bit stunned. Has my sister been picked up, did you say she was already taken?"

"Yes ma'am Simpson Brothers picked her up earlier today."

"Oh. Thank you. I guess that's all I needed to know." Janie's response was slow and measured.

"You bet. If you need the address I have it here." A few minutes later Janie hung up, the address for Simpson Brothers Crematory scribbled hastily on a piece of scrap paper from her purse. Her mind raced. She needed to stop that cremation. Better to go in person than try to do it by phone. She prayed she was not too late as she scrolled through her phone for the number of a local taxi. It was probably faster to phone and order one than stand on the sidewalk trying to flag one down. She paced as she waited. She needed to think about how she was going to stop the Funeral Home from cremating Clarissa. Could she be in trouble if she did that? Was she breaking any laws? *What the heck,* she thought, *I've probably broken a zillion laws already by accessing Ken Jones' email and bank account.*

Soon the taxi pulled up near the crosswalk to Temple Square and she quickly shut down her laptop, folded the wheely and awkwardly shoved everything into the back seat. After climbing in and giving the driver the address she sat back to rehearse her story. She closed her eyes and silently rehearsed what she was going to say and do. Twenty minutes later the driver pulled up in front of a red brick building with a simple sign reading Simpson Brothers Crematory. The lawn was neatly groomed but didn't have the typical shrubbery she associated with Funeral Homes. She paid the driver and got out, then re-assembled her wheely and laptop. Slinging her purse over her shoulder, she grasped the wheely handle and took a deep breath before starting her walk to the front entrance. The wind was picking up and whipped her hair around her face but she knew a disheveled appearance would fit the role she was about to play. Flying dirt and grit stung her face and made her eyes water. *Even better!* she thought.

A soft chime sounded as she opened the front door. Thick gray carpet the color of dirty clouds lined the floor and matched the slightly darker gray of the walls. The air-conditioning was going full blast and icy air played around her face. She shivered in the coolness. Dim lighting gave a hushed somber air to the small room. Piped in music played softly. Janie recognized it as something New Age with lots of tinkling bells and lapping waves in the background. Lutes added to the carefully planned mood of tranquility.

Her first thought was how small the room was. A large mahogany desk sat facing her and almost filled the entire length of the east wall. An assortment of urns sat on a set of shelves lining the south wall. A rather large young man sat behind the desk with two overstuffed dark green armchairs facing him. His dark hair was scrupulously clean and neatly trimmed. His freshly scrubbed face smiled gently as she walked towards him. With his necktie of dark somber blue in stark contrast to his gleaming white shirt he appeared as a beacon of light in the dimly lit room. Dark pants completed the outfit. He stood, then walked around the desk and waited quietly. When she reached him, he said in hushed tones, "Good afternoon. I'm Frank. How may I help you?" He gestured her to sit in the closest armchair.

Janie did not sit as directed. Instead she remained standing. "I'm here about my sister Clarissa Jones. I understand you picked up her body earlier today for cremation?"

The young man moved behind his desk. "Let me just check my records. Yes we did pick up Ms. Jones earlier today. I'm very sorry for your loss. Your sister is here and we'll take good care of her."

"So you've not cremated her yet?" Janie questioned him.

"No, Ms. Jones is scheduled for later this afternoon."

Janie's voice was sharp and decisive. "Then you must stop the cremation immediately!" His face registered surprise and his eyes opened wide. "Stop? But why? I'm afraid I don't understand."

"My brother had no authority to authorize cremation," Janie assured him. "He did this without our permission and it was not what my sister wanted. So you will stop the cremation immediately."

The young man's discomfort was obvious. "But I can't do that. Mr. Nelson paid in full for cremation and he's expecting to pick up the ashes tomorrow afternoon. It's all arranged."

"What part of stop are you not getting?" Janie's voice was haughty. "My brother did not have permission to do this. He doesn't have power of attorney and he's not the executor in the will. Did you check any of this with him before you took his money?"

"Well, no, I guess not," spluttered Frank "I mean, everything seemed in order, Mr. Nelson filled out the required papers and gave us the money up front and said he'd be back tomorrow for her ashes." He began rifling through his papers. "Yes, see, here it is, he filled out all the paperwork as required by law." He turned the papers towards Janie.

She did not look at them. "That may very well be, but he didn't have the legal authority to do so." She emphasized the word legal. "He isn't the executor, my older brother is, and he's flying in from England to make the proper arrangements for our sister. I would think you'd want to see those power of attorney or executor papers before continuing."

His face paled slightly. "Yes of course, we comply with all state laws. We certainly don't want any problems but your brother paid in advance for these services."

Janie's voice raised and she forced a stern look on her face. "Okay let me make myself perfectly clear. If you go ahead with this cremation, you'll have a lawsuit slapped on you and your firm so fast your head will spin." His face blanched. "Now, I suggest that you put a hold on this cremation until my brother arrives. He's the one who has the legal authority to say what's to become of my sister Clarissa's body. Then you can look over the papers he'll have with him. You'll see that he's the only one in the family who has the legal right to make any decisions regarding Clarissa."

She waited. He had slumped into his chair and was beginning to sweat. "Ma'am I'm sorry, we didn't know. I'll put a stop to the cremation. When did you say your brother will get here? We don't have a lot of room in the back and I need to know how long I might have to, umm, store your sister's body."

"Ted's flying in from England tomorrow and should be here sometime the day after that. But if he's delayed for any reason, I strongly advise you to forget about cremating my sister until you've seen the legal documents."

Janie was growing exhausted from keeping up the pretense. She was worried she was going to slip and make a mistake, say something that would arouse Frank's suspicions. *C'mon Frank* she thought, *say the right thing so I can leave!*

As if he could read her thoughts, Frank suddenly picked up his desk phone and made a quick call. "Ernie? Hold off on the cremation on Clarissa Jones. She arrived this morning but we're not doing her now." Janie sat down at last in the previously offered chair. She'd done it! She'd stopped the cremation, now she had to get the police involved. Without getting herself in trouble.

"That was a smart decision Frank," she stated with what seemed like perfect composure. Licking his lips nervously, Frank ran a stubby finger under his shirt collar to loosen it. "Yes. We don't want to cause any trouble Miss. I didn't know there was a problem. Please accept my apologies."

"Not a problem Frank. When my brother arrives I'll give him your name and phone number and he'll contact you. Meantime just sit tight and make sure no one cremates my sister." Standing, she turned on her heel and left the office.

27

When she was safely outside she paused and tried to steady her breathing. *Wow that was harder than I thought it would be! Never knew I was such a good liar. Hopefully I'm as good an actress as I am a liar.* She checked her Mickey Mouse watch pinned inside her purse. There was just barely time to contact the police and fill them in on her suspicions before meeting Steven for supper. She needed to freshen up first back at their hotel.

The hotel room smelled of cleaning solutions and fresh sheets and towels. There was no sign of Steven so she had time to make a few phone calls. She stood for a few minutes at the side of the bed, brow furrowed, as she debated whether to stretch out on top of the flowered bedspread or turn it down. Janie hated sitting on hotel bedspreads. Even in the cleanest hotels, she was pretty sure they were rarely, if ever, washed. But stretching out on the sheets in her street clothes, especially after having visited a crematory, gave her what her grandmother called the heebie-jeebies. Making her decision, she retrieved a couple of towels from the bathroom, placed them over the bedspread and carefully placed herself on top of them. That should do it, and she could always get more towels from housekeeping.

With her iPhone at her side and the Salt Lake City phonebook on her lap, she thumbed through it for a number to call for the police. She wasn't sure what their reaction would be, or even what she would tell them, but she was determined to alert them to the very strong possibility that someone in their city had been murdered. A half-hour later, after being put on hold several times and transferred to three different people, she spoke to a Detective who took her name and details of the crime. She was surprised that he knew about Clarissa's death but he informed her that Homicide Detectives reviewed all ambulance calls. Clarissa's had been noted but the review was not complete. After asking only a few questions, he'd suggested she come in and talk to him. So tomorrow morning first thing Janie would be on her way to see Detective Rankin in Homicide. She hung up with a sense of relief. If the police investigated she was sure that Ken Jones would soon be going to prison. A glance at the bedside clock showed her that she needed to get moving if she was going to meet Steven at 6:30.

A quick shower, vigorous toweling of her shaggy hair followed by a superficial blow-dry, minimal make-up, and she was ready to get dressed. Glancing out the window she noted that it was quite windy and somewhat overcast. She wanted to wear something a little nicer than what she wore for researching so decided on her ankle length platinum denim jeans. They fit like a glove and Steven loved how she looked in them. She topped them off with one of her favorite tees in pewter. Classy but not too dressy. Tiny pearl earrings and gray dress pumps completed the look. Last but not least in Janie's mind was her purse. Purses were her passion and she allowed herself free reign where they were concerned. She didn't smoke, she didn't drink, but buying expensive purses was her indulgence. At home she had dozens to choose from, but she'd only brought two with her to Salt Lake. Just as she made her decision, her cell rang and she answered it to hear Steven's voice.

"Hey babe, where are you right now?"

"Almost ready sweetie, I'm in the hotel room but I'll be out the door in five."

"Okay, sounds good, I'm already at the restaurant so I'll see you when you get here."

Janie swiped a bit of mocha colored lipstick over her mouth, checked her hair one last time, grabbed her sweater and was out the door headed for the elevators in less than the promised five minutes. Leaves were blowing on the trees, turning upside down in the wind and she thought she smelled a hint of rain in the air as she waited outside the hotel lobby for her taxi. Steven had made reservations at Cucina Toscana, a wonderful Tuscan Trattoria with Italian food Janie loved. Her mouth was already watering thinking about their delicious Asparagus Ravioli. Homemade pasta, great service, and a relaxing evening were in order tonight.

The taxi dropped her off in the parking lot behind what looked like an old warehouse. Steven was leaning against the railing outside waiting for her. He looked comfortably at ease in a green and gray striped short sleeve shirt, gray casual pants and a summer straw Fedora. His eyes lit up when he saw her. "You look beautiful," he whispered, as he leaned in to give her a brief kiss. They walked hand in hand through the restaurant doors and were soon seated at a small table for two. Janie eyed the arrangement of candle, salt and pepper and other items, then quickly shifted each a few inches away from her table setting. Steven was so used to her habit of rearranging restaurant table settings that he said nothing. Over cold drinks they shared their days. Their server Enrico was discreetly invisible, interrupting only to inquire about their orders. After making sure that there was nothing she was allergic to in the meal she wanted, Janie ordered the Monalisa Jacamoni Soup made with zucchini, potatoes, and asparagus, to be followed by her favorite Ravioli. If she had room she'd think about dessert later. Steven opted for the Cannellini bean soup as his appetizer, with a main course of pork tenderloin in green pepper sauce. They clinked glasses and carried on with their conversation. Steven was looking forward to the Art Gallery Show and for a moment Janie felt regret that she was not going with him.

The noise level in the restaurant was loud enough that Janie knew she'd have to raise her voice to share her adventures with the crematory and the police. She also knew she'd probably have to tell Steven at some point. Another of her Grandmother's sayings came to mind - *Least said, soonest mended. No sense spoiling a nice evening out,* she thought. Janie smiled at Steven's excitement over his visit to the Airplane Museum. He loved airplanes and was enthusiastically describing them to her in great detail.

After supper and a final cappuccino to finish the meal off, they walked hand in hand to their hotel. It was a cool evening but Janie was glad of the chance to be out in the fresh air. Steven was going to take a taxi from the hotel to the Art Gallery and Janie needed to grab her research notes. She decided that for the few hours left tonight before closing time, she was going to clear her mind completely and concentrate on her own genealogy. The wind was picking up as they walked and Steven commented that this was probably what the locals called the Monsoon effect. It could turn nasty but these July storms were usually short-lived.

At the hotel entrance, they kissed goodbye and Steven ran to a waiting taxi while Janie hurried through the lobby to the elevators. She didn't bother changing as there were only a few hours left before the library closed. A few minutes later she was on her way through the back alley to the library.

28

Settling into a vacant reader carrel, Janie studied her notes on her 4th great-grandmother and checked her research log. Her to-do list was not as current as she would have liked so she took another few minutes to jot down where she needed to look and the time frame. After a half-hour of prep work, she went to the library computer area to check their online catalog. She could then find out what films were available for the churches she needed. All she needed to do was search in that specific locale for churches, copy down the film numbers and start retrieving them. If there were a lot, she could print the pages instead and cross off each one as she finished the film.

There were enough that Janie didn't want to waste time writing them out so she inserted her copy card and hit the print key. She cursed silently. Her card showed that more money was needed and that meant she had to pick up her notes, head to the copy card machine and fish around for money, then go back and do her lookup over again. The library was starting to empty and a look at her watch showed it was already after nine o'clock. Only 50 minutes left before they closed, but maybe she could get one film done in that time. As she neared the copy card machine she saw Birdman, still in his long black trench coat, at the Information Desk. He seemed agitated and kept pushing a piece of paper towards one of the volunteers. This time Janie kept walking, determined not to edge closer to hear the conversation. She wanted to relax for tonight and do her own research.

It seemed only a few minutes later when she heard the announcement that the library was closing in fifteen minutes. She hadn't found anything new but could check off one of the churches from her list of items. Rewinding the microfilm always took awhile so she put her research notes away, shut down her laptop and began to crank the handle. It was always easier for her to rewind the film while standing so she stood up and leaned forward. Just then she caught a glimpse of a tall well-built man wearing a baseball cap and standing very still at the end of a row of readers. Her hand froze on the handle. She was pretty sure it was the same man who she'd seen yesterday carrying a photo around in his hand. He seemed to be looking at her, but as she strained to make out his face, he turned and strode quickly towards the elevators. Was he watching her?

Janie finished rewinding her film and putting it away. Gathering her papers, she left the 2nd floor and headed for the front doors. It was starting to rain but that was not unusual for Salt Lake in July.

Pausing in the tiny outer foyer, she searched as best she could for her travelling umbrella or rain jacket. She knew from previous trips that thunderstorms often occurred in the early evening. Although they didn't last long they could bring hail, lightning, and flooding in the streets.

The street was deserted. A few people scurried down the sidewalk, heads down and holding whatever they could find over their heads in a futile effort to stay dry. Thunder rumbled and the wind was beginning to pick up. Giving up on the idea of an umbrella or jacket, she decided to make a dash for it. It wasn't far to the alley and her hotel and she might make it before the storm hit with full force. There was no one in sight now and it seemed most people with any common sense had taken shelter until the storm passed.

Head down, she opened the door and began running clumsily for the main street. Her wheely bumped along behind her, tilting crazily with each step. By the time she turned the corner into the dark alley the wind had picked up. Intermittent flashes of lightning showed her the way to her hotel. Before she'd gone more than halfway down the alley, the wheely tipped and with a splash lodged itself in a puddle. Cursing, Janie bent to right the damn thing. A faint noise behind her caught her attention but before she could turn, she was shoved violently from behind. Her knees hit the pavement first and she yelped with pain. Her wrist bent backwards as she tried with an outstretched arm to stop her downward fall. For a moment she was stunned. Her rain-soaked hair tumbled around her face. Water dripped down her neck and back.

Her unseen assailant grabbed her wheely but could not wrench it away. Her arm had gone through the handlebars, effectively pinning it and her laptop with no hope of release unless her hand was forced off the ground. She leaned forward into her hand, letting even more of her body weight hold the wheely tight. Still on her hands and knees in the puddle, she began to punch backwards with her free hand. She heard a muffled curse as her fist connected with some part of her attacker's body.

Scream she thought. *Yell for help for God's sake!*

Suddenly her attacker grabbed her wrist and tried to wrench it backwards to free the handle of her wheely. Janie instinctively reached out with her free hand to grab his and felt her fingers close on something small and hard. A ring. She saw it glitter as she turned her head towards his hand. As frightened as she was, she noted the ring had a large dark stone in the middle and what looked like a bulldog on the side. She could barely make out some lettering around the stone - the last part looked like "ity" but in the struggle she couldn't see the rest.

"Stop! Stop that!" It wasn't her voice. For a brief moment she thought she imagined it but through the curtain of wet hair hanging over her eyes she saw a figure scurrying towards them, arms flapping wildly. "Leave her alone!" Her attacker released his grip so suddenly that she lost her balance and had to brace herself with her free hand again. By the time she turned her head, whoever had attacked her was gone, racing further into the wet darkness of the alley.

Janie was shaking from the rain and the attack. She tried to get up but stumbled as her bruised knee gave way. "Help me," she cried out, "I need help to get up." She turned her head towards whoever had saved her but he was not moving, still standing some twenty feet away. A flash of lightning overhead revealed an egg-shaped head and long dark trench coat. *Birdman!* Janie thought. *It's Birdman to the rescue!* She felt light-headed, even giddy. But her rescuer was not moving, he was just standing there watching her.

"Please, help me get up. I've hurt my leg." Janie was struggling to balance herself on her wheely handle so she could stand. Birdman's rough voice croaked "Are you okay?"

"No, I'm not okay," shrieked Janie. "I need help dammit! Why won't you help me get up!"

Another flash of lightning. She could hear feet pounding on the pavement. Birdman heard it too and with a whispered "I'm sorry," he flapped his spindly arms and scurried down the sidewalk, taking care to keep to the shadows. Janie could feel sobs welling up in her throat but she fought them down. A man and woman ran down the alley in her direction. "Oh my goodness," the woman called out, "are you okay?" The man with her reached Janie and extended a hand to pull her to her feet. Janie took a step and winced in pain, but managed to limp to the hotel with the young couple's help.

"You poor thing," said the young woman, "It's so dark and slippery in that darned alley, no wonder you fell."

Janie opened her mouth to protest but thought better of it and with chattering teeth, mumbled "Yes, clumsy me, I was trying to outrun the rain. Serves me right!"

29

A concerned desk clerk asked if she needed medical attention but she shook her head no. All she wanted was to go upstairs to her room, have a hot shower and lie down. Against her protests that she could manage, a bellboy was summoned to escort her. With shaking hands she extracted her key card, thanked the young couple and limped to the elevators with her escort. He kept up a running flow of conversation about the weather and what bad luck it was that she'd fallen, he hoped she was okay, her knee was bleeding, and on and on it went. Janie closed her eyes and leaning her head back against the elevator wall, wished for a speedy ascent. Soon she was at her door, thanking the bellboy and offering him a rather generous tip that he accepted with no hesitation.

Inside the safety of her room Janie allowed a few tears to flow. Part of it was relief that she was okay, part of it was anger that someone had dared to attack her and try to steal her laptop. She loved Salt Lake and had never had anything like that happen before. It was the safest city she had ever visited.

Stripping off her soaking wet clothes, she ran the water in the shower as hot as she could bear, then stood under it for several minutes. It felt so good to shampoo her hair and wash the grime and dirt from her body. She inspected her scraped knee. It was bruised and beginning to swell but it was a minor injury. However her wrist was already quite swollen and she thought it might be sprained. She'd send Steven to the drugstore to buy a tensor bandage if she had to. No big deal. What was a big deal was that someone had attacked her. She felt much calmer now, able to think clearly.

Salt Lake was a very safe city. She'd been here dozens of times, had walked alone from the library at night to the hotel. She didn't believe that it was a coincidence. Her attacker had not made any attempt to grab her purse which was dangling loosely on her other shoulder. That would have been an easy hit. Credit cards, cash, cell phone. Most women had at least that in their purses. Any robber with half a brain would have snatched her purse and run. They might also have tried for the laptop to sell it but no way would they make the laptop their main focus. *Think it through Janie!* She scolded herself silently.

Was it a random mugging? Or was she the intended target? If so then who was her attacker? One of the men she'd seen in the library? It wasn't Birdman, he'd yelled when he saw the attack and whoever pushed her down had fled. And whoever it was, he'd worn a gold ring, maybe a University or fraternity ring. That would fit with the letters "ity" she'd seen in the alley.

"Hi sweetie, I'm back!" She heard the hotel room door open at the same time as Steven's booming voice announced his arrival. The next thing she knew he was in the bathroom and had opened the shower curtain far enough to see her.

"Mmmm now that's what I call a treat! Want me to scrub your back?" His voice was a teasing whisper but quickly changed when she turned to face him. "My God Janie what's wrong? You look like hell!" His eyes took in her pale face, eyes swollen and red from crying and her scraped knees. A look of concern swept over him. "Did you fall? What happened?"

Tears welled up in her eyes again. She reached for a towel and stepped out of the shower. Her voice shook. "I was mugged. Outside in the alley."

Steven was horrified, and insisted they call the police but Janie shook her head. "No. No Steven I need to tell you some things first." She put on her nightgown and wished she'd packed a robe but her old sweater would have to do.

Steven peppered her with questions while she sat on the sofa and towel dried her hair. Over the next hour she filled him in on most of what she'd done over the past two days. Seeing the look on his face as she rehashed the past two days' events, Janie was glad she was keeping a few things from him – like going through Ken's email and bank accounts and going to the crematory.

Steven couldn't stop himself. "What the hell do you think you're doing Janie? Going to this man's office? What were you thinking? He just lost his wife and you're tracking him down to face off with him? If he's a killer you've put yourself in danger. If he's not, you've made a damn nuisance of yourself."

"It wasn't like that Steven. I figured I could get a good sense of whether or not he had anything to do with Clarissa's death if I was face to face with him."

Steven's voice rose. "For God's sake Janie you're not Sherlock freaking Holmes! You're a 54 year old grandmother from Connecticut. You're sticking your nose in where it doesn't belong and annoying everyone." He tossed his Fedora on the bed in exasperation. "Didn't you learn your lesson in St. Lucia? You almost got yourself arrested and charged with harassment that time."

"Sherlock Holmes?" Janie swallowed to stop from laughing. "Did you compare me to Sherlock Holmes? Wow, that's a compliment." But Steven was having none of it.

"Dammit Janie. You think you're some kind of damned detective and you go off half-cocked trying to solve some imaginary mystery. Every time we go somewhere something like this happens. It's too much Janie." He ran his hand across the top of his head, a worried frown on his face.

"Steven, you know I don't go looking for trouble. But it seems to find me."

"BS!" Steven cut her off. "You go looking for trouble. Remember in St. Lucia? What happened there? You chased someone around for an entire day because you thought there was something suspicious going on. And you almost got arrested by the local cops because of that little stunt!"

Janie snapped back "Okay I was wrong about St. Lucia but don't forget what happened in England. Someone was murdered and I was right about who did it. Same with this thing. A woman died right beside me. I know there's more to it. Someone killed her and I'm betting on her ex as the person who had a hand in it. If he didn't kill her, maybe he hired someone to do it."

"Sweetheart, I worry about you. If you're right and this mugging tonight is connected, then you've put yourself in danger. If this mugging was just a co-incidence, then at the very least you've made yourself look like a stalker and you've managed to piss people off. Your degree in Psychology doesn't make you an expert in human behavior!" He stopped in mid-sentence and shook his head. "Why do I bother? I know you, once you've decided on a course of action, there's no stopping you. I give up. I'm going to get some Peroxide and a tensor bandage for that wrist. Do not leave this room Janie. Lock the door behind me and make sure you stay put. Can you do that one thing?" The sarcasm in his voice was not lost on her. She closed her eyes and hoped that he'd be slightly less annoyed by the time he got back.

When he returned and completed wrapping the tensor around her swollen wrist, Janie reached out to touch his hand. "Steven I'm going to get the police to investigate so there's no need to worry about me. I've got no reason to keep checking into Clarissa's death."

Steven adjusted the tensor bandage on her wrist before fastening it. "You know, I see your lips moving and I hear your voice but for some reason I don't believe the words. I haven't forgotten England and that's why I'm concerned." He sat back, looked into her eyes and sighed. "Janie one of the reasons I fell in love with you was because of your spirit and your passion. But this determination you have to right the wrongs of the world, or maybe I should say the perceived wrongs of the world, is a bit much. Maybe it's time you stopped being a Crusader for justice."

"Don't be annoyed with me and don't scold me for goodness sake. I'm me. I'm who I am, I've never pretended to be anything else and you knew it before you got down on your knees over hot dogs on bread and asked me to marry you." She saw a twitch in the corner of his mouth. He gave a wry grin.

"Hot dogs and bread. I guess it wasn't the most romantic well-planned proposal was it? But boy oh boy if you'd told me then what I was getting myself in for, I might have thought twice about it!"

Janie leaned forward and kissed him. She loosened her hold on the sweater that she'd draped around her shoulders. "No you wouldn't, you'd be lost without me." His response was immediate and the kiss deepened.

"Damn you Janie, you know I can't resist you," he whispered in her ear as his fingers slipped the straps of her nightgown off her shoulders. Her negligee fell to her waist and she leaned back against the sofa cushions as he kissed and caressed her. Slowly she gave in to his touch and put all thoughts of Clarissa and her death on hold.

30

New York City May 12, 1880

Katie bit her lips to stop from screaming. Another contraction hit hard. Sweat rolled down her face and chest. She'd been in labor for six hours now and was exhausted and frightened. Mrs. Teadley had been kind about letting her stay on once she found out that Katie was with child. "Girl as long as you can do your work, I could care less," Mrs. Teadley said, and that was that. The Missus of course took no notice of the servants, and one pregnant Irish girl was of no interest to her.

And now here she was, in her tiny bed in the attic room, trying hard not to scream as she drew closer to bringing her child into the world. Mrs. Teadley had even called the midwife who was now at the foot of her bed encouraging Katie. "Push now! That's it, that's a girl, push push push!" With a sudden surge of pain Katie felt the baby propel out and then a slap and a wail, tentative at first, but growing steadily stronger. "Right you are dear, it's a fine healthy boy" The midwife wiped the child down with an old towel, and placed him on Katie's heaving belly. "Take him to your breast dear, that's the way to do it."

Katie felt a rush of love like no other she'd ever felt, not even for the baby's father. A sweet baby smell drifted up to her nose and she smiled as she gently touched his soft baby cheeks. She took him to her breast and inspected his fingers and toes as he suckled. "What will you call him dear?" asked the midwife as she busied herself cleaning up the bloody rags and sheets.

"Samuel after my father," replied Katie. "Samuel Jacob. Samuel Jacob Donnelly." She said his name aloud, trying it on for size.

"A fine name dear, and one I'm sure he'll be proud to carry."

She gave Katie instructions on feeding, bathing and changing little Samuel's diapers, then she held her hand out for her wages. "Ta dear, lovely helping your son into the world." With a slight wave of her hand she was gone.

Katie touched the gold locket she had pinned to her chemise. He couldn't be with her for the birth, and in fact he'd been distant since she told him she was bearing his child. But the locket brought her comfort. As she brought Samuel to her shoulder to burp him, he hiccupped and a tiny bubble of her breast milk ran out of his mouth. Katie used the embroidered hanky given to her by her ma to wipe his little chin then tucked it under his chin to use next time he spit up.

If only Joey were here! But he had not replied to her last letter sent four months ago. She told him that she was with child and who the father was. She knew Joey would be furious and would beat her lover within an inch of his life if he could get back to the city, but she prayed he could not. She was expecting a response though and his silence saddened and frightened her. Without her brother, the only comforts she had were the hanky from mam and the locket from her lover. But now she had her beautiful son and no matter what, she would love him and take care of him. No one could take that away from her.

31

The harsh buzz of the bedside alarm pierced Janie's sleep-fogged brain. She opened her eyes slowly. When she moved her wrist it was sore and her knees were a bit raw but otherwise she felt okay. Rolling over, she tried to remember why she'd set the alarm. Oh yeah, she had to get moving to meet Homicide Detective Rankin by 9 a.m. Steven was grumbling from his side of the bed so she quickly shut the alarm off. Relief. She hated alarms and generally didn't need one, waking up naturally every morning between 7 and 7:30 a.m. Not that she had to get up that early. It was just her weird body clock. She rarely slept past 7:30 no matter what time she went to bed the night before.

Steven was the opposite, he'd sleep until noon if he didn't have to go to his antique store or meet with clients. Janie was one of those dreaded morning people. She woke up alert, happy and ready to start her day. Steven's morning ritual was quite different. First he took a half hour lying in bed after he woke up. Then a half hour sitting on the edge of the bed with his eyes closed. Then a forty-five minute shower, during which Janie was sure he was sleeping. Then an hour sipping a cup of tea while reading the news until finally he was awake enough to start on his day. Luckily for Steven, he could pretty much set his own hours. His successful antique store catered to a higher end clientele and was only open by appointment. But it was his following of wealthy clients who needed him to acquire a must-have piece of art that brought in the real money. Janie often thought how lucky he was, how lucky they were, to have lucked into such a great lifestyle. They weren't rich by any means, but they were comfortable, and they were their own bosses.

Janie stood in front of the foggy hotel mirror. Her hot shower had managed to steam it up so that she had trouble seeing her image. Thank goodness for good genetics! Her mother and grandmother had looked much younger than their ages and those genes seemed to have passed on down to Janie. Since Steven was some fourteen years her junior, she hoped she never looked her actual age. With practiced strokes, Janie applied a touch of eggplant powder to her eyelids and blended it well with the highlighter she'd applied to the top half of her lids. Dark eyeliner on her upper lid followed by black lash lengthening mascara finished up her eye makeup. A touch of blush on her cheeks and magenta lip gloss on her full lips completed the look. She worked some gel into her feathered cut hair and pulled up a few strands of hair here and there for the slightly wind-blown look she preferred.

She gave some thought to what to wear. It was important that the police take her seriously. She decided her casual dress slacks in a light gray, topped with a short sleeve black top would be perfect. Nothing fancy but the outfit exuded confidence and class. She hesitated briefly but then decided earrings only, no necklace, no dangling bracelet. Simple was best. Classy but simple. She'd tame her hair down a bit too. Top it all off with just a touch of makeup and she'd be set.

Steven looked up as she finished dressing. "Going somewhere special?" he asked. "That doesn't look like your usual research outfit."

Janie knew she had to tell him. She braced herself for his reaction "I'm going to the police this morning to report Clarissa's death."

His eyes opened wide. "What?? Are you crazy? What do you think you can tell them they don't already know? Older woman drops dead in street. Probable heart attack. End of story!"

She shook her head. "I plan on telling them about her being followed, about her ex-husband harassing her, about her briefcase being stolen, about her purse missing, and anything else that seems suspicious."

"Janie, those can all be explained logically. You're going to look like an idiot if you go traipsing off to the police with that."

Janie's voice took on a brittle edge. "Steven you cannot explain someone claiming to be her brother picking up her purse at the hospital, claiming her body, and then having it sent off for cremation. It's all very suspicious and I'm going to let the police know about it."

Steven flung back the bedcovers, sat up and rubbed his head. "Janie, I've no idea what gets into you sometimes. Although

104

actually I guess I do. You can't let go, can you?" His voice softened, became gentle. "Sweetheart, you can't keep doing this. You can't bring your dad back. You don't need to atone for his death by trying to right every wrong you think you've uncovered. It won't solve his murder. And it won't help you come to terms with his death."

Janie's face paled. Her lips trembled as she spoke. "That's unfair and you know it. I don't want to talk about this, or about my father. I'm doing it because Clarissa deserves better than to be written up as a natural death. She was murdered. I'm absolutely convinced of that, and you know I've been right before. I trust my little voice."

She turned away and began gathering her purse and a sweater. "I'm going for breakfast now. I have a 9 a.m. appointment and I don't want to be late."

Steven reached out for her. "Hon, let's not argue okay? I worry about you, that's all."

"Don't keep trying to change me Steven." Janie was unrelenting. "I'm me. I'm not you. And I'm doing what I feel is the right thing to do whether you like it or agree with it or not. As you're so fond of saying – end of story."

He shrugged. "Okay, have it your way. I'll try to keep my mouth shut from now on but I'm not making any promises." He stood and held out his arms. "Hug before you go?" Janie could never stay mad at him for long. She moved into his arms and returned his hug. He kissed her cheek and said quietly "Call me when you're finished with the police okay? Just so I know you're okay. We can figure out our supper plans then too." With a wave and a forced smile she was out the door. She'd go to a nearby diner for breakfast then take a taxi to the police station. She was looking forward to talking to this Detective Rankin and wanted to think about how much she was going to tell him.

32

The taxi ride did not take long and soon she was standing outside the police station, pausing before going in. She needed a few seconds to gather her thoughts and compose herself before facing Rankin. Once inside the building Janie went directly to the Information Desk and stated her name and who she was meeting. She took a quick look around and was impressed by the scrupulously clean furniture and fresh decor. To her relief she did not have to wait but was immediately directed to Detective Rankin in Homicide. She was pleasantly surprised to see a clean-cut middle-aged man in a brown tweed sports jacket, light blue shirt with chocolate brown tie, and neatly pressed beige slacks. His balding head still had a bit of graying hair which he had combed over to try to disguise the thin spots on top. His name splate confirmed who he was, and Janie extended her hand. "Detective Rankin? I'm Janie Riley, we spoke yesterday about Clarissa Jones."

He reluctantly stood, shook her hand with an overly firm grip, and indicated she should be seated in the chair closest to her. He took a seat behind his desk and pulled out a form and a pen. "Okay Ms. Riley, what did you want to tell me about Mrs. Jones and her death?"

Over the next half hour Janie filled him in on the suspicious events surrounding Clarissa's death. She left out her own part in going to Ken Jones' office, hacking into his email and bank accounts and going to the crematory to stop the cremation. At first he listened intently but within a few minutes he was peppering her with questions. A few times he broke in before her sentence was complete. After several of these interruptions Janie stopped, took a deep breath and with an edge to her voice said, "Detective I would appreciate it if you could save your questions until I'm done. It breaks my train of thought to have you constantly interrupting me."

His face registered surprise and then anger. A red flush appeared on his cheeks. "Ms. Riley, you're here for my help so I think you better get used to how I do things."

Janie felt her own face going pink with anger. "Can we continue please? I'd like to finish up and get back to my research."

"Do you want us to investigate or not?"

"Of course I do!"

"Then I need answers, but if you don't wanna give them..." He shrugged. His expression made it clear he didn't care one way or the other. Janie swallowed her angry words. Gritting her teeth she said quietly, "Fine, ask away." His smug expression was not lost on her, but she needed him to file that report.

More questions. She responded as best she could. He listened, interrupting a few more times to clarify her words or ask for more detail. When she told him about the Private Investigator showing up after Clarissa's death and telling her that she was being watched, he showed real interest for the first time. "Do you know who he was?" he asked.

Janie fished in her purse. 'Yes, I have his business card here." She handed it across the desk and saw a flash of what looked like recognition on Rankin's face as he read the name.

"Never heard of him," he said, tossing the card back to her.

Janie hid her surprise. She was silent for a long moment then said, "What happens now?"

He didn't answer her question but instead leaned back in his chair. "What's your connection to the deceased Mrs. Riley?" He waited for Janie's response, his dark blue eyes never leaving her face.

"I'm a friend. I met her a few days ago when I first came to Salt Lake."

His eyes narrowed. "And what's your interest in her death?"

Janie hesitated. "Other than not wanting someone to get away with murder? Nothing really except Clarissa seemed like a nice woman and she didn't deserve to die."

Rankin continued eyeing her, sizing her up. Janie could feel the heat rising in her face under his scrutiny. "Is there a problem?" she asked. She believed that the best defense was an offense and she didn't want too many more questions, some of which she couldn't answer without getting herself in trouble.

"No problem." His answer was curt.

"What about her body? It's still at the crematory and I doubt they'll hold it forever." She thought she caught a flash of curiosity cross his face but he quickly rearranged his features into a poker face.

"We'll have her picked up and taken to the Coroner's Office until our investigation is complete."

"Will there be an autopsy?" she pressed on.

"Most likely. That's up to my Supervisor." He stood, indicating the meeting was over. "Thanks for coming to us with this information. We'll contact you if we need anything further."

Janie stood as well. "Will you call me when you find something?" A look of annoyance crossed his face before he could hide it. "We don't normally do that."

"Then I'll call you." Janie's voice was firm.

His phone rang and he turned to answer it. Covering the mouthpiece with one hand, he spoke to her. "Fine, call me in a couple of weeks and I'll let you know where we're at." He sat down, swiveled his chair around and barked into the phone, "Rankin here. What's up?"

He watched Janie leave, made his excuses to whoever was on the phone, and hung up. Casually he left his desk, walked across the room and looked down the hallway to make sure she was gone. Returning to his desk, he fished a cell phone out of his belt and chose his contact list. A few rings later his call was answered. "Hey Kenny boy, it's Rankin. We need to talk. I think we have a problem."

33

Janie walked briskly outside and waited for a taxi. Once she was in the car she heaved a sigh of relief and fell back against the seat cushions. She hadn't liked Rankin's attitude but was pleased that the Detective seemed to take her seriously and that the police were going to look into things. A huge weight was lifted from her shoulders and maybe now she could concentrate on other things.

On the ride back to her hotel Janie thought about last night. Why had Birdman run off? Why was he in the alley during the storm? Did he know who attacked her? She had lots of questions and was determined to get answers. No way was she letting him run off this time, he was going to answer her questions. But first she wanted to use Google to find the ring she'd spotted on her attacker. Maybe she could find it online and if so, she'd have more details about the man who knocked her down.

A quick change of clothes in her hotel room and Janie was ready for the library. But first she fired up her trusty laptop and started her search for the ring by using the keywords "university ring bulldog". She'd start with that and then move on to the word fraternity if she had to.

Her search brought up too many hits so Janie decided to find a site that sold university rings. If she saw images of them she was pretty sure she'd recognize the one her attacker had worn. After a half hour of searching she spotted it. It was a class ring for Yale University made of gold with a dark blue stone on top surrounded by the raised words Yale University. On the side was a bulldog. *Bingo*, she whispered aloud. *What kind of mugger wears a Yale ring?* Her brow furrowed in concentration then she gave a sigh and shut her laptop down.

She'd have time to think about the ring later but for now she needed to get to the library. But first a quick stop at the vending machine to grab a couple of bottles of water. She didn't like having to leave her research area to go to the Main Floor Snack Room to buy water during the day and she hated using the public drinking fountain near the bathrooms. All she could think of when she used one was how many people might have touched the fountain with their mouths. Or sneezed on it. Her germ radar was always on full alert in public places.

Locking her hotel room door, she hurried to the elevators and out the back entrance to the alley. Walking briskly through the alley she found herself glancing over her shoulder. She couldn't stop thinking about last night and wondering why someone would attack her and try to take her laptop instead of her purse.

It was chilly outside and she wished she'd put on her sweater. Not wanting to take the time to stop and retrieve it from her research bag, she continued on, walking even faster. By the time she got to the library doors she was shivering. Her cold feet were already making her regret her decision to wear her open-toed black sandals. They were super comfortable but also stylish, which is why she'd chosen them but the damn strap kept slipping off her heel and her toes were like ice. Now she wished she'd opted for her more practical running shoes. She crossed her fingers that her travel socks were in her research bag. She always took them on airplanes and they'd warmed her feet many times during an uncomfortable plane ride.

Smiling and returning the warm good morning from the volunteer at the front doors, she headed for the elevators where she shifted impatiently from foot to foot while she waited with other patrons just as eager to find their ancestors. Nods and smiles were given and returned. Accidentally running her wheely over another researcher's foot as they tried to enter the elevator at the same time, Janie apologized and moved as far away as possible. The doors opened and like lemmings they surged out to occupy carrels and desks and computer tables.

She wondered if Birdman was here, and if so, on what floor. Her plan was to put her laptop and research binder in one of the lockers on the 2nd floor, then start her search. To Janie's relief, her usual carrel was empty. Having found this microfilm reader to her liking she wasn't keen on having to hunt for a new one. She hurriedly put on her sweater and fished out her socks for her icy feet.

Now to find Birdman. Janie began at the microfilm readers, walking along the end of the four rows, eyes looking left and right, slowly scanning for Birdman's recognizable long trench coat. She could miss him if he were sitting at a reader, but she'd go back only if she needed to and walk up and down each row. Not spotting him, she moved on to look down the rows of microfilm drawers. That was harder to do as there were places where she could miss seeing someone. Nothing she thought. What if he's not here today? Then what?

Rounding the end of the last row of microfilm, she stopped. Wasn't that the same man she'd seen a few days ago, the one she first saw wearing expensive clothes? She'd seen him the next day, dark stubble on his face and wearing what looked like hand-me-downs, including a shabby dirty baseball cap. But she was sure that was him even though he was back in his expensive clothes with his face freshly shaved. No dirty baseball cap, no torn pullover. He was hunched over one of the computers. Curious, she edged a bit closer, and caught a whiff of unmistakable expensive cologne. She kept moving and as she passed the end of the computer row, he looked directly at her then quickly averted his eyes, put his head down and stared at the monitor. She waited for a moment, and then saw him take another furtive glance in her direction. *Weird,* she thought. *Her grandmother was right - it took all kinds.*

34

Janie continued her search but Birdman was nowhere to be found. Her next place to look was the 3rd floor US/Canada books and with that in mind she headed towards the elevators. When the doors opened she found herself staring right at the man she wanted. Birdman and several other researchers were on the elevator. As the elevator emptied, Birdman saw Janie, did an about-face and backed back into the car. He began frantically punching buttons and the elevator doors began to close. Janie quickly thrust out a hand between the doors and pushed her way into the car. Blocking the exit as Birdman scrambled to get past her, she spread her arms wide. "No you don't! You're staying right here. I want to talk to you."

The elevator began its slow descent as Birdman backed into a corner, his mouth open but no sound coming out. He looked terrified and Janie forced herself to speak gently. "It's okay, I just want to ask you some questions." His Adams apple bobbed as he swallowed and his fingers began to flutter rapidly. Beads of sweat gathered on his forehead and his breathing quickened. "I want to thank you for helping me last night. In the alley." Janie backed slowly into the opposite corner, giving him plenty of space and keeping her voice as gentle as she could. His eyes flickered in her direction. He nodded his head. Encouraged by his response, Janie tried a smile. "Could we sit in the lounge area and talk for a minute?"

When the elevator stopped and the second the doors opened, Birdman slipped out, turning sideways in his rush to leave. Janie hurried behind him and touched his arm. "Wait," she whispered forcefully. "I'm not going to stop following you so you may as well come and sit with me for a minute. Just here in the lounge. See, there are some empty chairs over here." She pointed to two chairs in the seating area to their left.

He whirled around when he felt her hand on his arm and began backing away, his eyes wide. "Okay okay okay," he croaked. "Just for a minute." And with that he made a bee-line for one of the chairs. His long trench coat fluttered around him as he threw himself down and pushed his frame back into a corner of the chair furthest from the empty one beside him. Janie sat too and leaned back, trying to appear casual and non-threatening.

Birdman rocked forward, hunched over his knees and keeping his hands tightly clasped. "You gave me my lunch." His voice was hoarse as if he rarely used it. Janie looked at him quizzically. "At the airport. You gave me my lunch. I would have been hungry without it."

"Yes, I remember." Janie smiled. "I didn't want you to be hungry."

"Yea. That was nice. That was good."

Janie waited, unsure if she should speak or wait for Birdman to continue. "I'm Janie, what's your name?" she asked after several seconds had passed.

"Umm. Morris." he lowered his head and mumbled his name.

"I wanted to thank you for chasing that man away last night Morris. But why did you run away?"

Morris glanced at her briefly from under his stringy hair which was now falling around his face. He averted his eyes. "I was scared. He was hurting you but then I got scared so I ran. They do that you know."

"They? Who are "they" and what do they do?" Janie furrowed her brows, trying to figure out what he meant.

He raised his head then and looked around. Leaning forward he looked around once more, then whispered. "The Mormons. They lock up your stuff and won't let you find your ancestors."

Janie wasn't sure what to say. "Morris, That's not true. The Mormons set this library up so we could all come here and use their records. They want us to find our ancestors."

"No!" he was shaking his head violently now. "No, they won't let me see mine. They know I'm royalty, they know Charlemagne is my ancestor but they lock up my records so I can't prove it, and that means I can't have my money. I come here all the time and I look and I look and I ask them and they keep saying they don't know but they DO." He was becoming more and more agitated with each word. Spittle flew out of his mouth.

"That must be very upsetting for you Morris." Janie decided her best course of action was to make it sound like she was agreeing without actually agreeing. From his aversion to making eye contact, his social awkwardness and his flitting of his fingers when obviously stressed, she thought it a safe bet that he suffered from Asperger's Syndrome or something similar. She would have guessed Social Anxiety except for the wriggling of his fingers and bobbing of his head, repetitive movements that calmed those suffering from AS or autism. If it was autism he was very high-functioning. To keep him talking she had to make the situation non-threatening for him and not push too hard with too many questions. Any intensity from her could push him over the edge.

"I was wondering though if you could describe the man who pushed me down last night." Janie's voice was soft and gentle and she forced herself to speak slowly.

He shook his head several times. "Unh-uh. It was dark. I don't know him but he's probably trying to stop you from finding your money too."

"Well, I'm not looking for any money Morris. I just want to find whoever knocked me down. He tried to take my computer."

"Yep that's what they do. They take your stuff and they lock up your genealogy and they won't let you find your ancestors. That's what he was doing I think."

Janie took a breath. "Morris I know it wasn't the Mormons who attacked me. He didn't want my genealogy. He wanted my laptop. Tell me what he looked like, okay? What was he wearing?"

Morris shrugged and swallowed several times. "I dunno. I dunno. It was dark. I saw him and I yelled and he ran. Then I ran. But I saw him take that lady's genealogy so I know he was a Mormon and he was trying to take yours too."

"What lady? Tell me about that Morris." She tried to contain her excitement. What had he seen?

"The lady. You were with her. She got sick."

Janie sat very still. "Did you see something Morris? Something about the lady and the man who attacked me?"

"I told you!" his voice grew louder and people around them glanced their way. When he saw them looking their way he started to wiggle his fingers frantically and he bobbed his head from side to side several times.

"It's okay Morris. I just forgot for a second. Can you remind me again what you saw?"

"He took her papers. She went out with you and he took her ancestors from her desk. Then she was looking for them. I saw her looking and looking on her desk and in her case. But she couldn't find them 'cuz he took them. I saw him." He was whispering but his voice was getting louder.

"What did he look like? Where did he go? Did you follow him?" Janie's questions came out quickly, one after the other and Morris became more frantic. "Stop asking me! I dunno. I don't wanna talk anymore! I thought you were my friend but you're making me talk and it hurts my head!"

"I am your friend, Morris. I'm sorry. We don't have to talk anymore. Maybe we can go and have a nice cold drink downstairs. Would you like that?"

"No no no. I don't wanna talk anymore! I gotta go now" He was shaking his head rapidly and sweat was dripping from his forehead and running down his cheeks. "I'm all done, I gotta make them unlock my ancestors so I can get my money." Morris stood and headed off in the direction of the Reference Desk. Janie had her mouth open to say more but he left quickly before she could get the words out.

35

She sat there feeling bewildered. Trying to make sense of what Morris had told her, trying to separate reality from his wild fantasies. This had something to do with Clarissa's death. She was sure of it. Someone had stolen Clarissa's research notes and that same person had attacked her last night in the alley and tried to take hers. *Think Janie!* She scolded herself. *Slow down and think this through!*

The police were investigating Clarissa's death. They were almost certainly checking out her ex-husband very carefully. But they didn't know about Clarissa's research notes being stolen, or Janie herself being attacked. Janie wasn't sure she wanted to let Detective Rankin know. She might pursue this new lead herself. Janie also hadn't told Rankin about the phone call Clarissa made during her research. None of that had seemed important. Her main concern was to stop the cremation and get Ken looked at more carefully. For a moment she felt guilty – should she be telling the police everything, including her part in stopping the cremation, going to the hospital and Ken's office?

After several minutes of thinking things through she made her decision. She was not going to the police with these new facts. She was not going to reveal her part in reading Ken's email and checking his bank account. She'd do what she did best, which was to keep searching for more clues. She wasn't sure if Clarissa's research fit into her death, but the only way she was going to find out was to figure out who Clarissa was working for and what she was researching.

Having made up her mind, Janie retrieved her laptop and notes from her locker and made her way to a microfilm reader. First things first, probably the easiest thing to do was to take a look at what Clarissa was working on. The newspaper page wasn't much help to her at this point. Then she remembered the papers she retrieved from Clarissa's microfilm reader cubbyhole. She had not returned them to Clarissa. That was a stroke of luck since all Clarissa's research notes were now missing.

Rummaging through her research bag she crossed her fingers

that the papers would give her some kind of clue. Bingo! There were two pages. One was a computer printout from the 1880 New York City census. There were five families listed. The households contained servants as well, and there were 50 names on the page. Each individual had their age, birthplace and occupation listed, as well as the birthplace of their parents. The second page she'd meant to return to Clarissa was from New York Vital Statistics showing marriages, but it had been badly copied and was partially off the page. Clarissa had probably meant to toss it out and simply forgot it was tucked in her cubby-hole. Janie couldn't read everything on it, much of the text had been cut off, so she set it aside for the time being. The census page seemed a much better place to start.

The New York Times newspaper page that Clarissa had been looking at just before she died had dozens of names. Janie decided to check each of those names against that 1880 census page to see if any were the same. All of the homes had servants so it must be a fairly well-off area of the city. It was for households on 5th Avenue in Manhattan and had been taken on the 3rd of June. She ran her finger down the list of names: Keenan, Doyle, Nolan, Watts, Hamelin, Corbin, Willard, Keegan, Allen, Skelly, Kilfoy, Deluge, Whitestone, McMahon, Rice, Donnelly, Teadley, Alcott, Walsh, Bugley, Brewer, O'Brien, Cunningham, Stevenson, Gladey, McDonaghue, Durran, McMahon, Rice, Chapin, Davis. Nothing jumped out at her. Many were stock brokers. There was a physician, a few merchants, a jeweler, clergyman and a lawyer and many servants. Trying to figure out which one was the focus of Clarissa's research was going to be tricky.

After an hour of comparing names on the census to the newspaper page, she decided she wasn't getting anywhere. So far none of the names were a match. Maybe she needed to find each person from the 1880 census page in another census year. Since the 1890 census was missing, she'd have to go backward to 1870 because going ahead twenty years to 1900 wouldn't likely be much help. Unless there was a state census for 1885. Janie cursed her own inexperience with 1880s New York records. She'd have to find out what state census records existed. Better yet, she'd just log into Ancestry on the library computers and search for each of the names from 1880.

As she hurried to the library computer station she made a mental checklist of what she knew and what she needed to find out. Her grandmother used to say *You can't see what's under a woodpile until you lift the logs one at a time, girl.* She might be lifting logs to find nothing but she wouldn't know until the logs were cleared away.

36

Janie's head was spinning. She'd found many of the individuals from 1880 in the 1870 census but nothing was coming clear for her. She was just gathering a lot of family details on each one. She needed to take a break, clear her head and figure out where to go from this point. She couldn't keep researching all of these families, it was far too many. She needed to hone in on Clarissa's person or persons of interest. Gathering her printouts from the computer, she made her way slowly to her microfilm reader carrel. She wanted to take her laptop with her. After last night she wasn't comfortable leaving it unattended for long periods. Especially if someone was watching her. The thought made her shiver and she felt the hairs on the back of her neck stand up.

Pulling her wheely behind her she headed for the bathrooms. Glancing to her right she saw Birdman standing at the Reception Desk. Morris she reminded herself. His name is Morris. Hesitating for a moment she paused, then changed direction. Reaching the desk she stood off to one side. Morris was engaged in a heated conversation with a pleasant faced middle aged volunteer. The volunteer's strained smile showed her level of discomfort as Morris berated her "You've got it, you know you have, why won't you give it to me?"

"I really don't have it but I'll be glad to help you find it" the woman said. Janie edged closer then gently called out "Hi Morris." She waited. He swallowed several times and cast a sideways glance her way. "They won't give it to me."

Janie nodded her head "Let's get a cold drink Morris. Take a little break, okay? Then maybe we can get you set up on a reader and you can look through some films. Okay?"

"Will you help?" came his reply.

"Sure I will. But let's get a cold drink right now. I'm thirsty."

Morris turned away from the desk and started towards the stairs. "I don't like the elevator today, I like the stairs."

Janie had to walk quickly to keep up with him. It was going to be difficult to get her wheely down a flight of stairs but she couldn't risk leaving Morris. It took some pushing and kicking with her right foot but she managed to bump the wheely all the way down to the main floor where Morris was pacing impatiently. He'd scurried down so fast it was impossible for her to keep up.

"Where were you? I've been waiting a long time."

"I'm sorry Morris, it took me awhile to get down the stairs. But I'm here now."

"I'm thirsty. Do you have my drink?"

"Not on me. We have to go to the Snack Room."

Morris made a face. "I don't like Snack Room. Too many people."

"Well then you wait here and I'll go get your drink and bring it back here." Janie looked outside. "Do you want to wait outside for me?"

Morris nodded his head and turned to go.

"Wait Morris. What do you want to drink? Soda? Water?"

"I like orange soda. It's pretty good." Morris' eyes darted from one side to the next as he edged closer to the exit. Janie wasn't sure he'd wait but she had no choice. Several frustrating minutes passed while she struggled with the vending machine but eventually she had Morris' soda and her water. She heaved a sigh of relief to see him sitting on the concrete wall around the flower bed in the courtyard.

"Here's your soda Morris." She sat down a few feet away from him being careful not to invade his personal space. He took the soda without a word, popped the top and began drinking greedily.

"So, do you live nearby?"

He wiped his mouth with his sleeve. "Nope. I came on an airplane. I need my ancestors but they won't give 'em to me."

"I'll help you with that if you want. But tell me about your first day at the library. What did you do all day?"

He shrugged his shoulders. "I dunno. I looked for my ancestors. I told the Mormons I wanted them but they got 'em locked up. I walked around."

"Did you see anyone you know?"

"I saw you. You were with the lady who got sick."

"Anyone else? Did you see a man looking at us?"

Another shrug. "Maybe."

"Can you tell me why you were watching us, Morris?"

"Watching who?" he looked at her from the corner of his eyes.

"C'mon Morris, I know you were watching my friend. Or watching me. I'm not mad, I just wonder why."

He hesitated slightly. "Well, promise you won't get mad?"

"I promise Morris. Cross my heart." Janie made a cross with her fingers over her heart.

"Okay. I thought she was pretty. She looks like my sister. But I wasn't going to hurt her. I just wanted to look at her."

"That's okay Morris. She was pretty. What about the next day? Did you see a man watching us?"

"Yep. He grabbed her arm and yelled at her."

Janie kept the frustration from her face. He was talking about Ken. "Anyone else watching?"

"Well, maybe not watching but another man took her ancestors. I forget what day he did that, but she kept looking, and you looked too. He just walked right past her desk and he grabbed them and kept walking."

"Yeah, that's the guy. What did he look like Morris?"

Shrug. "I dunno. He was walking fast."

"What was he wearing? A coat? A hat? Jeans? Sweater? Close your eyes and try to picture him."

Long silence. Morris closed his eyes. Suddenly they popped open. "Hat. A baseball hat."

Janie hid her excitement. "That's great Morris, thanks. Did you see him any other times?"

"Yea, lots of times. He was hanging around the library looking for his ancestors."

"Anyone else? Did you notice any other people?"

"Sure, yeah. Lots of people here looking for their ancestors but the Mormons are keeping them from all of us." He swallowed the last of his soda. "I'm thirsty."

"Okay, I'll get you another drink in a minute. Tell me about the guy who pushed me down in the alley."

He shook his head. "Already told you. It was dark. And rainy. He was all dark and he shoved you. So I yelled and he ran. Then I ran." He stood up. "I need a drink, I'm going now."

Janie reached out a hand to stop him. She realized her mistake but too late. He recoiled. His mouth worked, his eyes darted frantically from side to side and his hands flapped. "Morris, wait!" But he was gone, scurrying to the light and across the street to Temple Square.

Good going Janie. Scare the poor guy off.

Her cell phone rang early the next morning. Stumbling out of the shower soaking wet, and wishing she'd packed her cozy warm bathrobe, she fumbled for her cell and slid the bar to answer. "Ms. Riley?" A strange male voice spoke. "It's Detective Rankin. I thought you'd like to know that I've gone over the notes I made when you were here yesterday and I'm checking into your friend's death."

Janie felt the tension drain out of her body. Pushing back her wet hair from her flushed face she exclaimed, "I'm so pleased! Are you doing an autopsy on Clarissa's body? And checking out her ex-husband?" "Yep," came the gruff response, "You don't need to worry about a thing. I'm on top of it. One thing Ms. Riley, if you have questions make sure you call me directly. I'm in charge of the case and no sense you trying to get answers from anyone else. They'd just blow you off or put you through to other detectives. You can reach me at the number I'm calling from if you need anything."

Janie paused, hand in mid-air on its way to wrap her towel more tightly around her shivering body. *What was with this change of heart and attitude,* she thought. *Yesterday he's a cold fish but today's he's Mr. Nice Guy.* "Ms. Riley, you there?" Detective Rankin was waiting for her response. "Oh yes sorry Detective I'm here, and I appreciate your kindness."

"Yeah, sure thing," came his response. "Don't worry, I'm taking care of it." And with that he hung up. Janie wasted no time getting back to the bathroom where she could towel off and get her clothes on. The phone call had roused Steven from his sleep and he was already stirring.

"There. That should do it." Rankin turned to Ken with a smirk. "That should get her off your back."

Ken leaned back with a frown, his office chair creaking as he did so. "I still don't like it. If she keeps nosing around she might find out what we're up to. We can't risk it!"

"Nothing more I can do." Rankin shrugged and snuffed out his cigarette in the overflowing ashtray on Ken's desk. "As long as she thinks I'm investigating the death and that you're the number one suspect, she'll be happy. And she's only visiting so she'll be gone soon and then we'll be okay. Meantime, just lie low for a few days until she's gone." He rose from his chair, his large frame almost filling the office. "And one other thing. Clean this damn pigsty! It stinks."

Janie shivered as she dressed. Her grandmother always said that when you shivered it meant someone had just walked over your grave. A bemused half-smile appeared on Janie's face as she pictured her beloved Grandma giving in to such a superstitious belief. Steven's muffled voice jolted her out of her musings. "Hey hon you almost done in there? I'm starving!"

"Coming," she yelled back. "Just have to dry my hair."

Over a hasty breakfast of barely edible fried eggs and toast, Janie filled Steven in on her plans for the day. Making a face, she sipped her weak coffee, wondering if there was a good coffee shop nearby so she could get a decent cup. "Disgusting! Steven you'd think they could at least cook fried eggs without having them so runny they end up too dreadful to eat!" The smell of her burnt toast was nauseating enough without watching slimy eggs sliding around on the plate. Steven gave a shrug and continued wolfing his breakfast down with no trouble. "Just get something else later Janie. Don't get all bent out of shape over a breakfast. Tomorrow we'll eat in the hotel restaurant, okay?"

Janie's hand froze in mid-air with her coffee cup halfway to her mouth. "Look Steven," she hissed quietly, "There's that Detective again!" She'd spotted Dan Mulroney just sitting down at a table across the room. Steven didn't turn his head to look, but she heard him give an exasperated sigh. "Janie." Her name was drawn out on his lips and she heard his accusatory tone. It was time to change the subject. After a few minutes of chatting about the weather, Janie smiled. "I'm off to the library, babe. See you around 6ish?"

Steven reached out to give her hand a gentle squeeze. "That's fine sweetie. Good luck with chasing your great great whoever down!" They leaned over the table for a quick peck on the lips, then Janie gathered her wheely and purse and headed for the door. She had to pass by Dan's table and she gave a tiny smile and nod of her head as she did. He gave a lop-sided grin of his own and raised his coffee cup in her direction. Then she was out the door and in the hot dry air. She sauntered along enjoying the smell of flowers and greenery, and the feel of the light breeze on her skin. It was a fifteen minute walk to the library but on such a beautiful day she didn't mind. In fact it was a chance to clear her head and puzzle over some of the events of the past few days. Janie liked to visualize a problem as a mind map in her head. She pictured each clue and event in boxes that she moved around in her head, linking clues and people and unexplained happenings together. She found that helped her to figure out solutions or the next step to take.

Absorbed in her thoughts she didn't notice a black SUV slow down as it approached the intersection. She stood on the sidewalk waiting patiently for the familiar bird call to indicate when the light was in her favor. As soon as she heard it she stepped off the curb and began to walk a little faster. The streets in Salt Lake City were very wide and there wasn't much time to get across before the lights changed. She was almost at the half-way point when the SUV gunned its motor and headed in her direction. "Watch it!" She heard a deep voice at the same moment a strong hand roughly grabbed her arm in a vice-like grip and yanked her forcefully backward. Janie gave a scream as she stumbled back into whoever had grabbed her. The SUV sped by, missing her by inches, and continued racing down the street. She heard a male voice ask if she was okay. A shaken Janie regained her balance and twisted around to find Dan Mulroney holding her. His gray eyes probed her face and his lips had tightened. She nodded, unable to speak.

"Let's get you safely off the road," he said as he picked up her wheely and gently took her elbow. Cars that had stopped were now honking for them to move off the street. Dan gave them a wave of acknowledgment and guided Janie to the sidewalk. Pedestrians who had stopped to stare lost interest and went on their way. The sun seemed very warm and Janie realized her heart was racing and skipping beats. Sweat beaded on her forehead and she could feel it trickling down the back of her neck. *Adrenalin reaction* she thought. She was shaken but anger was also beginning to stir. "That's twice someone has tried to hurt me!" she exclaimed, her voice trembling.

Dan released her elbow and scrutinized her pale face for a few seconds. "Maybe you should tell me about it." His deep voice had a hint of concern and Janie knew she might burst into tears if he continued to be solicitous. But she needed someone to talk to and he seemed like a reasonable choice. She remembered the Mickey Mouse watch he wore. Surely anyone wearing such a watch was trustworthy. And he had just saved her life.

40

The aroma of freshly brewed coffee permeated the air as Janie and Dan entered the cafe. A bright cheerfulness filled the small room which held a few well-dressed customers dotted here and there. The hum of conversation combined with the clatter of dishes in the kitchen was a welcome sound. Ceiling fans stirred the air and wafted the sweet smell of cinnamon and apples throughout the room. Janie's stomach growled, reminding her she hadn't eaten much of her breakfast. Suddenly she was ravenous. She wondered if it was normal to feel so hungry after nearly being killed. Even if Dan thought she was a nut case she planned to order a big piece of homemade apple pie and a carafe of strong coffee.

Dan chose a table for two by a window. Wooden shutters covered the bottom half and delicate lacy half-curtains splashed across the top. A single yellow flower in a clear glass vase atop a blue-checkered tablecloth gave off a welcoming air. The bright sun streaming in added to the overall warmth. Janie liked that you could open or close the shutters and as soon as she took her seat on the overstuffed chair she began playing with them, adjusting them until the light was to her liking. After moving the vase with the flower slightly to the left so that it was in the center of the table she sat back and tried to relax.

They didn't speak until a perky young waitress had taken their order. Janie realized she didn't feel uncomfortable with the silence. It seemed natural. Dan also seemed at ease and there was something about him that made Janie feel she was safe in his presence. She took the time to study Dan furtively. He'd missed a small spot on his left jaw when shaving this morning and she noted the tiny nick his razor had left. It was a strong jaw matched by steely gray eyes that assessed the room casually. He still favored worn jeans topped with a t-shirt. Today he was wearing dark green, a color that suited him. He ran a hand through his thick and slightly unruly salt and pepper hair before leaning forward.

Both started to speak at the same time. With a chuckle, Dan

128

gestured to Janie to go ahead. Taking a deep breath along with a forkful of steaming apple pie, Janie began. Dan's eyes never left her face and for the next half hour he listened attentively while she poured out her story. She left nothing out. His shaggy eyebrows raised and lowered a few times during the telling. Occasionally his left cheek tensed as his jaw muscles worked. But he did not interrupt the flow of her story and for that she was grateful. Finally she sat back and waited for his response. A sip of her now cold coffee caused a grimace to cross her face. Dan noticed and raised a finger to summon their waitress. Fresh hot coffee soon appeared. Janie sipped gratefully.

"That's strange about Rankin investigating so quickly after you talked to him. I don't know how he'd get approval that fast. Police departments don't work that way. Besides, I know him and he's not the kind to want to take on more work than the bare minimum required. And the autopsy results wouldn't be in that fast. It takes awhile to get one done and then it could take a few days for a toxicology report." Dan's brow furrowed as he sat in thought. Janie sat quietly, not wanting to interrupt his concentration but almost twitching with impatience. "Let me check into that," he said after a few minutes of deep thought.

Intense relief flooded Janie. "You believe me then that something isn't right? I'm convinced Clarissa was killed and I'm pretty sure it was her ex. But there's something else that bothers me. The ring. Why would Ken mug me and why would he be wearing a Yale ring? I didn't notice one on his finger when I was in his office and he doesn't exactly strike me as Yale material. And why did the mugger only want my laptop? Why not my purse? And you just said you know Rankin but when I told him your name he said he never heard of you!"

"Yep," Dan agreed. "Rankin's not exactly the most truthful guy around, plus he doesn't like me. If we look at all the facts a lot of things don't add up. But there's one thing I can do that might be helpful. If you want me to I can get a buddy to run a check on Clarissa's calls on her cell the day she was killed. He owes me a couple of favors." He'd been leaning over the table speaking in hushed tones but now he rocked back and took a huge gulp of his coffee.

"I can't pay you." Janie shook her head. "My husband would be ticked if I brought a Private Eye into this!" Her eyes darkened as her hopes began to die.

"Did I ask for money?" Dan sounded insulted. His jaw tensed. His voice took on a more urgent tone and he leaned towards her again. "You've been attacked once, maybe twice. A woman is dead. Someone appears desperate to get her notes and yours, or at the very least to get you out of the picture. That tells me you're on to something. And that puts you in danger. I'm not about to let that go." Janie's face flushed and she felt moisture welling in her eyes. Blinking hard and swallowing to hide her emotions, she nodded her head. "Thank you." She managed to squeak the words out without giving way to tears.

"Okay then we've got a deal. I do some leg work and you keep a low profile. That might put you out of harm's way. But there's one other thing - have you told your husband any of this?" Janie hesitated, unsure whether or not to tell him the truth about Steven's lack of involvement. *In for a penny, in for a pound*, her English grandmother used to say. Either she trusted Dan or she didn't. His eyes missed nothing and she knew she had to answer. She took a big breath and then she shook her head. "Steven doesn't like me getting involved," was all she said. Dan eyed her with one eyebrow cocked then nodded.

"Okay I'll walk you to the library and then I'll get started. You might want to give me your cell phone number so I can contact you." He waved away her offer of money for her share of the bill, took a worn wallet stuffed with pieces of paper out of his pocket and left a generous tip.

Dan walked her to the front door of the library, completely ignoring her when she protested that she could go alone. He left her with instructions to stay alert, be aware of her surroundings, and make sure she had people around her at all times.

41

When Janie finally settled into a carrel in front of a microfilm reader, her mind was whirling. She could hardly think straight but knew she needed to focus.

She was ready to continue retracing Clarissa's steps. *Slow and meticulous,* she thought to herself. *Just the way you always do genealogy research. Take your time, write down what you find, not what you expect to find, and let each fact and clue guide you to the next.*

First she decided to make a list of what she knew. She still preferred old-fashioned pen and paper for this part of the research process. There was something about the visualization that she just couldn't achieve on a computer. Digging into her worn leather research bag she rifled through a stack of papers until she found the New York Times page from July 1880 and the New York City census for 1880. Frowning, Janie studied the two pieces of paper for a few moments. She shifted in her chair and yawned with her mouth closed tightly. She needed to find a common thread among all these pages. Something caught Clarissa's attention and she needed to figure out what it was. A name. It had to be a name. She'd already checked the 1870 census for the names from the 1880 census page but there were so many names it grew onerous and nothing had jumped out at her. And no names matched on the newspaper page.

She remembered that Clarissa had seemed excited after reading a page from New York Births. *What was the date? Think Janie think!* she scolded herself. *What had Clarissa been studying?* Closing her eyes, she forced herself to shut out all distractions. Slowly the sounds of microfilm reader handles being cranked faded. She no longer heard reels of film whizzing on the spools as they were rewound, the soft whispers of staff or the creaking of chairs as folks settled in or stood up. An image of Clarissa seated at her carrel filled Janie's mind. It was fuzzy at first, like a photograph slightly out of focus. It was always blurry when she first tried to bring an image back to her conscious mind. Shutting out everything except Clarissa and the reader she slowly brought the scene into focus.

Details began to emerge from the fog. Clarissa's bright green belt. The soft pink sweater Clarissa wore that day. The stray hair lying on her shoulder that Janie wished she could pluck off. The immaculate white bob of her hair. Scattered on the carrel surface were papers, pens and pencils. At Clarissa's feet lay her Bosca briefcase. Her laptop was closed and in the cubby-hole under the carrel. The top shelf held two microfilms. Janie concentrated on seeing what was on the reader screen. She pictured herself standing behind Clarissa peering over her shoulder to read the page. The page was blurry. Slowly Janie forced it to come into focus. She could see a word here and there but not the complete page. The start of a smile broke out as the focus sharpened and she saw the heading May 1880 splashed across the top of the page. Then it was gone.

Janie sat back in her chair, exhausted. She knew a headache would follow, it always did after one of her intense sessions. Forcing herself to rest, she took a few gulps of water from her water bottle, then closed her eyes again and breathed deeply. Her forehead was beaded with sweat from the strain of such intense concentration and she wiped it with her free hand. Soon she was checking the online catalog for the film number for the records of births in May 1880. A few minutes later she had the correct reel and was headed back to her reader. Her hand flew as she cranked the worn handle of the microfilm reader to get to May. Controlling her impatience she decided to print a copy of all the births registered in that month. There were hundreds but she figured that would be the easiest way to check for a matching name from either the 1880 census or the newspaper page.

After a quick visit to the copy room, she hurried back to her reader and spread the pages out as best she could in the confined space. There were too many pages of May births to fit them all on the desk so Janie decided to examine them one page at a time. Reaching out, she arranged the papers in chronological order. 1880 census, all May 1880 births and lastly the July 1880 newspaper page. Taking a deep breath as her excitement mounted she began to study the names.

After an hour her pounding head and uncontrollable yawns dictated it was time for a break. Some fresh air and coffee might rejuvenate her waning enthusiasm for the task. So far there'd been no matching names and she was growing discouraged. She could almost taste a Starbuck's cappuccino and wondered if she should walk to the nearby Radisson, get a take-out, and then head back to the library. The two block walk might clear her head. And she didn't feel like another cup of bad coffee from a vending machine.

Didn't take much to convince you my girl she thought. With that she zipped her laptop in her carry bag, checked that she had her purse and headed to the elevators. She didn't feel like packing up all her papers and figured she could get away with leaving them for the half hour she'd be gone. The attendants smiled in her direction as she passed and Janie forced a big smile of her own. Once out the front doors she stopped in surprise. The smell of damp grass and earth told her that while she'd been cooped up in the library it had rained. As her eyes adjusted she realized a light drizzle was still coming down. She wished she'd remembered her folding umbrella but it was back in the room. Did she feel like walking those two blocks in the rain? A jolt to her back as a patron bumped into her told her she better step aside and make a decision.

42

Coffee was a definite must. Her decision made, she began walking briskly towards the corner. The maple trees lining the sidewalk gave some cover from the drizzle and the smell of damp flowers and grass was refreshing. She could feel the tension draining from her back and neck as she walked. Breathing deeply and slowly she concentrated on relaxing her mind and body. Soon she was at the front door of the hotel and through the revolving doors. The usual hotel lobby odors of furniture polish and leather greeted her as she passed through on her way to the small gift shop tucked away in the corner. Seeing the empty couches near the bar she regretted leaving her papers behind. It would have been nice to sit and sip her coffee while looking through the records.

It didn't take long for one large steaming cup of cappuccino to be produced by the young man behind the counter. Janie headed back to the lobby, already anticipating the first sip. Sighing she sank down on the oversized couch and took a gulp. Closing her eyes she savored the moment, enjoying the heady aroma of coffee beans and cream. Within ten minutes she was ready to head back to the library. *Batteries recharged,* she thought, *and good to go!*

The ringing of her cell phone jolted Janie out of her musings and she began rummaging frantically through crumpled tissues and assorted bits and pieces of paper in her over-stuffed purse. By the time she found her phone buried at the bottom under some candies and her makeup bag, the caller had hung up. A glance at the missed calls showed Steven's name. A quick call back and they confirmed dinner at 8 p.m. He had some potential clients to meet with and needed time to convince them to purchase some fine art pieces. It always amazed Janie that no matter where they went, Steven always managed to find a few people willing to spend big bucks on art.

Back at the library she quickly got to work, studying each page of the birth records carefully, checking for any match to a name on the 1880 census page. Several hours later she stretched, yawned and leaned back in her chair, brow furrowed in puzzlement. Nothing matched. She absent-mindedly scratched her forehead then began twirling her pencil between the fingers of her right hand. She knew she'd checked each name carefully. Something should have matched. How on earth would she ever figure out what Clarissa found if she didn't know what name to research?

Idly she flipped through the dozens of pages. Perhaps she'd missed one. There was always a chance two had stuck together. Laying them out she began to check page numbers. Could she have missed one when she copied them? She shook her head slightly. She was always super careful about copying every page. But there it was. One page was missing. The numbers jumped from page 32 to page 34. Where was page 33? She went through the pile again. No page 33. That was strange. Janie knew she was obsessing about the missing page but that was her way. She didn't like discrepancies and was compelled to solve them when they arose. *If Steven were here he'd tell me to forget about it and just get another copy of the damned page,* she thought.

It didn't take long to find page 33 on the original film and copy it, then go back to her desk to read the names of children and parents. Using her finger she slowly traced down the page, unwilling to take a chance that her eyes might accidentally miss a name. Her lips moved as she mouthed the names on the page. Sanderson. Jackman. Holmes. Van Valkenburg. Donnelly. Smith. Her finger hesitated. Went back to the line above. Donnelly. That sounded familiar. She blinked her eyes to clear her vision then scrutinized the 1880 census sheet. Loomis, McKing, Baldwin, Vanderbilt, Kelley, Banks, Moran, Keegan, Whitestone. Whitacre. Teadley. O'Brien. Cunningham. Donnelly. Donnelly! Janie's excitement surged and she read the entire entry:

Katherine Donnelly, 18 years old, servant, born Ireland. The next line showed Samuel J. Donnelly, 2 months old, born New York.

Janie's eyes darted back to the page of birth records. Anyone who knew her would have realized that her flared nostrils and wide open eyes meant she was on to something. Her finger flew down the page to stop at the fifth birth recorded on May 12,

1880. It was for Samuel Jacob Donnelly born that day in Manhattan. Little Samuel's mother was listed as Katie Donnelly. Katie. A nickname for Katherine. The father's name had been recorded but then scratched out heavily with black ink. Janie had never seen a name inked out before. It wasn't a single line as a clerk might do if he goofed and put a name in the wrong spot. It looked like a deliberate attempt to hide the father's name. Janie took out her magnifier and studied the inked out part. She could just make out some tall strokes above the horizontal ink lines. One had a loop at the top so was probably b, f, h, k or l. The second was a sharp straight line and Janie decided that could only be d or t.

It looked like Katherine Donnelly, the Irish servant girl, had an illegitimate son named Samuel Jacob. *Wonder who the father was*, Janie thought idly. She continued reading the census page. Katherine was a servant in a big house situated on 5th Avenue. The head of the house was listed as Jacob Whitestone, 41 years old, born England. His occupation was given as a manufacturer and he was living with a wife Augusta and young son Charles, as well as five servants, one of whom was Katherine Donnelly. Janie was impressed. *Must have been a rich guy to have so many servants! Wonder what he manufactured.*

An old Jimi Hendrix song playing full blast startled her out of her reverie. Disapproving glares from other patrons let her know she'd forgotten to mute her phone again. This time she managed to find it fairly quickly. She whispered a soft greeting as she answered. To her surprise it was Dan asking if they could meet tomorrow for coffee. He had news for her but didn't want to talk about it over the phone. They arranged to meet around 10 a.m. at the same coffee house they'd been at this morning. After hanging up she glanced at her Mickey Mouse watch and realized she was going to be late meeting Steven. Gathering her papers and stowing her laptop on its wheely, she threw her purse under one arm and strode off, hoping she had time to freshen up at their hotel.

43

Over the start of their meal at Olive Garden, Janie filled Steven in on most, but not all, of her day. *Better leave out the part where someone tried to run me down. And Dan and I having coffee,* she decided. His eyebrows raised in disbelief when she started to explain about the missing page of birth records, then finding the birth and the name of the father being obliterated. "C'mon Janie, that's nuts! Are you seriously telling me you think someone took one page of those records off your desk? And that they somehow blacked out some record from 1880?"

"Steven, no of course not! Whoever blacked that out in 1880 was most likely a clerk. Maybe the father bribed someone in the register office. But yes, I think someone might have taken page 33 from my carrel while I was at the Radisson."

Steven's exasperation was evident from his sigh. "You probably missed copying that page." Janie shook her head. "I don't think so. What are the odds that the page with the matching names from the census would be the one page I miss in almost forty pages?"

"For God's sake Janie, it doesn't always have to be some deep dark conspiracy! Sometimes a cigar is just a cigar. No hidden meaning, no mysterious secret." His fork clattered on his plate as he dropped it beside his half-eaten salad. "You know, you always manage to do this. We go on a vacation and you get all caught up in some nonsense about murder or whatever. Why can't you ever just let it go? When do we get to have a conversation that doesn't include you telling me someone's dead and you're on the trail of some unknown killer?"

"Because I know what I saw!" Janie didn't try to hide her frustration.

Steven's body tensed as he leaned back in his chair, his meal forgotten. "Forget it. I can see you're determined to make something out of nothing. So fine, go ahead, but I'm tired of hearing about it."

The arrival of the waiter with their dinners put an end to the heated conversation. Even the wonderful aroma of her chicken in garlic and rosemary couldn't lift the heavy knot Janie now had in the pit of her stomach. They ate in silence. Their disagreement hadn't affected Steven's appetite and he attacked his shrimp dish with enthusiasm. Janie picked aimlessly at her meal, forgoing her usual Tiramisu and cappuccino treat after dinner. Forcing a smile, Janie finally spoke in a quiet voice. "I don't want to fight Steven, but you know I have hunches and gut feelings and I've been right before. I can't let someone be murdered and not do something about it."

"Fine," was Steven's curt response. "Just keep sticking your nose in where it doesn't belong. You'll do what you want anyway, no sense my trying to give you good advice." With that he slapped his credit card down on the bill and gestured for their waiter, who had been hovering nearby, to take it. Janie's lips tightened with annoyance but she decided silence was best. She could almost hear her grandmother's voice - *Least said, soonest mended.*

The walk back to their hotel was filled with tension and unspoken words. Just before they reached the hotel front doors, Steven reached out for Janie's hand. "Sorry," he mumbled, "but I worry about you. And I want some time just with you, not with all the suspicious people you see." Janie squeezed his hand in acknowledgment and leaned in for a light kiss. "I'm sorry too. I don't mean to exclude or worry you. And I'll be careful, I promise." Steven shook his head. "I don't want you to be careful. I want you to stop." Reluctantly Janie agreed even though she knew there was no way she could stop now.

The strident tones of Steven's ring-tone broke the silence that followed Janie's slight nod of her head. Reaching into his pocket, he checked the call display and with a slight groan, answered with "This is Steve." Silence at his end as he listened intently. Janie continued on into the well-lit lobby where she decided to wait for him. She could see him standing just outside the doors. He was listening more than talking but his arm and hand movements seemed to indicate that this was an unwanted call. After a few minutes of agitated conversation he put his phone back in his pocket, stood for a moment then joined Janie where she sat on the lobby couch. "Anything wrong?" she enquired. "I'll tell you in the room," came his gruff response. He seemed annoyed as he led the way to the elevators.

Steven broke the news to her after they'd gone inside their room and settled on the comfortable couch in the corner. "I've got to go to France," he said bluntly as he took her in his arms. She started to snuggle in but stopped and sat up with surprise. "France! Why? When?" Pulling her back down he explained that his new client insisted on a specific sculpture that was in a gallery in France. He'd have to negotiate the deal in person and needed to leave as soon as possible. She had a million questions but Steven was not in the mood to listen. "Not now." His voice was husky and his lips moved softly on her neck. Soon she gave in to his gentle but insistent kisses.

44

Steven was not in bed when Janie woke the next morning. Groggy from their late night, she yawned and stretched before sitting slowly up. Usually she was awake long before him. The aroma of coffee and after-shave filled her nostrils. Blinking and rubbing her eyes she saw that Steven was seated at the small desk, toweling his wet hair with one hand while the other danced between Janie's open laptop and a cup of steaming coffee. Turning, he smiled at her "Good morning sleepyhead. Want some coffee?" He gestured at the in-room coffee pot that was still half full.

She nodded and waited while he fixed it just the way she liked it. Taking a tentative sip after first inhaling the delicious smell, she finally spoke. "How come you're up so early?"

"Gotta find a flight to Paris, babe," came his distracted response. He fished out a credit card from the wallet lying on the desk, and fingers flying on the keyboard, entered information then closed the laptop and sat back. "Okay sweetie, I'm booked on an 11 a.m. flight this morning. I'm already packed so just have time to get dressed and get going. I'll grab some breakfast in the airport." He was already up and headed for the bathroom. Leaving the door open he continued talking while he added a quick swipe of gel to his unruly hair and a finger combing to set it in place. "I'm sorry I've gotta rush off like this but I'll get this done as fast as possible and then I'll fly home and meet you there. I'll phone you when I get a hotel in Paris and let you know where I am."

He was at the hotel room closet door now and stepping into his favorite khaki pants, his green and yellow flowered short-sleeve button-down from Nordstrom's, and a light beige jacket. Checking his watch he strode to the bed where she was still sipping her coffee, leaned over and kissed her. "You okay hon?" he asked. She smiled. "I'm fine. I've got lots to do still. You go, make that client happy and don't worry about me. I'm a big girl now, I can fly home alone, no problem."

"Love you sweetie. Take care of yourself and don't get into

any trouble." Steven gave her a quick peck on the lips, his dimples flashing as he smiled. "Love you too, now get going! You're going to miss that plane!" Janie managed a quick squeeze of his hand before he turned to leave. He stopped at the door, suitcase in his hand and jacket slung over his arm, gave a sweeping glance to make sure he had everything he needed, then blew her a kiss and was gone.

Janie lay back against the cushions, relief mixed with guilt flooding through her. She would miss Steven but his absence meant she could do whatever she needed to do without trying to hide it from him, or defend herself against his disapproval. Throwing back the covers she experienced a renewed sense of purpose. Today was the day she'd dig deep into online records and figure out what Clarissa was working on. Even if it didn't connect to her death, Janie was determined to retrace Clarissa's work. Often some little fact turned out to be the clue you needed, whether in genealogy research or when looking for a killer.

A quick shower, minimal makeup, and letting her hair air-dry while she dressed helped Janie speed up her morning routine. It looked hot outside even at this hour, so she chose her beige capris which were not only comfortable but cooler than her black pair. Scrutinizing her choice of tops, a wine-colored v-neck short sleeve shirt from Joseph Ribkoff caught her eye. She knew the color suited her and even better it always brightened her spirits. She gulped the last of her now-cold coffee as she hurried into the bathroom to style her hair. Five more minutes and she'd be ready. All she needed was a bit of setting gel. She didn't want to take the time to eat a full breakfast so rummaged for the crackers that she always carried. She could grab a late breakfast when she met Dan.

Powering up her laptop she pulled out her research plan from her binder. With a quick study of her notes on what to do first, she logged on to the online library catalogue and made a list of film numbers she needed. Since the library was closed today she would look online for Katie and little Samuel in the 1900 census for New York.

Logging on to her favorite census site, she began her search but soon realized they were nowhere to be found. She found the house where Katie had lived as a servant in 1880 and jotted down names and particulars of the household in her notebook. The Whitestone family still occupied the house but Katie was not listed. Of course it was a twenty year gap between records so no doubt Katie had moved on or was married. But it was odd that she couldn't find Samuel. He'd be about 20 in 1900. She wondered if there was a state census for New York anytime in those missing years.

A quick search indicated there were no state census records but there was an 1892 police census. She read about the database and soon learned that it was an enumeration of twenty-four districts in New York County taken by the New York City Police in September and October of 1892. Her excitement rose. Manhattan was in New York County. There was a good chance she might find Katie or Samuel listed. She began her search but after a few minutes raised her eyes from the monitor. Nothing. She was disappointed but not discouraged. A big part of genealogy research involved going down roads and following clues that led nowhere. Setting her laptop aside she collected her thoughts. She would start at the one item that she hadn't yet managed to connect to the 1880 census and the 1880 birth records. That New York Times newspaper page from July had to be studied again for clues she might have missed the first time.

It didn't take long to find the newspaper page, and Janie began slowly reading the headlines again. This time she also read any stories that looked like possible connections to Katie and Samuel Donnelly. She often found that following a hunch or making an educated guess was a productive method of research. It paid to look under all stones and not leave anything to chance. Her eyes stopped at the story of a man charged with the murder of a prostitute. She couldn't see an immediate connection but mentally filed it away as a possibility.

Another few minutes of study and she stopped at one story that grabbed her attention. After reading the story twice she carefully copied it into her notebook.

A Pauper at 2 Months Old
John Van Slyke of Seventh Street who was enjoying an evening

perambulation with his wife, found an abandoned male infant about 2 months old on the steps of a home at St Mark's Place. The child was handed over to authorities and will no doubt join the estimated 200 children abandoned every year and sent to the Children's Hospital on Randall's Island. The foundling's only identification was a lace hanky with the initials K.D.

Janie's heart was racing and her face flushed. *K.D. That could be Katie Donnelly's hanky,* she thought, *which meant that the abandoned baby was almost certainly little Samuel!*

She tried to contain her growing excitement. It was only a hunch, a theory that she needed to follow to either prove or disprove. Her first step would be to find out if records existed for the Children's Hospital mentioned in the article. With a tiny bit of luck she might find an admission record for the baby. Perhaps there would be more details that the newspaper hadn't printed. But her mind was whirring. Why would Katie abandon her two month old son? Did she marry? Die? Was she simply unable to care for him? What happened to Katie?

Janie checked her watch. She still had time before meeting Dan and with any luck she'd find the Hospital records had survived and were on microfilm. *Please please please,* she thought to herself as she opened her laptop to check the online catalogue. Bingo! There were various records dating from 1851 to 1935. She quickly skimmed the list of available films, ignoring records of foundlings, parents, and adoptions but stopping at records of admissions from 1863 to 1900. She wanted to find out if the abandoned child had been admitted after being turned over to authorities. Jotting down the film number she filed it away for tomorrow when the library was open, then decided she might as well check Cyndi's List to see if the records she needed were available online. Sure enough the records for the Children's Hospital were listed, and a link directed her to the website.

The records had no index and with a small sigh, Janie resigned herself to scrolling through each image. She reached July 7th before spotting him. It was a brief admission note written in a cramped spidery hand but Janie was used to reading old handwriting and had no problem deciphering the notation.

July 7, 1880. 2 month old male child, well-nourished. Found abandoned at 76 St. Mark's Place by J. Van Slyke. 1 lace hanky initials K.D. with clothing. Name assigned: Kendall Duggan. Remarks: Discharged May 12, 1884 to care of Mr. & Mrs. John Vrooman of Mulberry Street

She sat back in her chair, a pleased grin on her face. *Gotcha my boy!*, she thought. If this was little Samuel Donnelly he'd ended up with the name Kendall Duggan and when he was four years old was sent to live with John Vrooman and his wife. She needed to check that 1892 police census again for the Vrooman family. And there they were. John Vrooman age 52, his wife Fanny age 50 and Kendall Duggan age 12, adopted child. Janie was on a roll. With this information she could trace Kendall Duggan and hopefully find out what happened to him. Janie had no idea if this was connected to Clarissa's murder, or if Kendall Duggan was little Samuel Donnelly but that wasn't going to deter her. She'd learned long ago that you never ignored a lead, no matter where it took you. It didn't matter if you could connect the dots at the start of your research, you just noted your facts carefully and kept on looking!

Jimi Hendrix was singing his song again and she quickly slid the bar to answer. Expecting Steven's voice, she was surprised to hear Dan's. "Hey there, did you forget about meeting me?" Her eyes opened wide and she glanced at the time. 10:21. "Sorry!" She shifted the phone to her shoulder while quickly using one free hand to shuffle papers and stuff them into her leather bag and the other to shut down her laptop. "I got sidetracked. Give me 10 minutes okay?" She could hardly wait to tell Dan what she'd found, and to hear what news he had.

45

The tantalizing smell of fresh lemon wafted towards Janie as she opened the cafe door. Soft chimes announced her arrival and a smiling hostess headed her way. Spotting Dan at a table in the corner, she shook her head and pointed in his direction. He looked up from his phone, gave his lop-sided grin then pointed to his watch. "I know and I'm so sorry. But I was onto something and forgot about the time." "No problem." he shrugged. "I got some work done while I was waiting."

Janie settled into a chair. "I've been meaning to ask you something. Do you have Native American heritage?"

Dan looked startled. "Why do you ask that?"

Janie rushed to explain. "Well I have a Mohawk ancestor and I'm interested in Native American history and you have a certain look that makes me think you might have Native American heritage too."

Dan laughed. "You sound like you wish you hadn't asked."

Janie blushed slightly.

Dan grinned. "It's okay. The answer is yes. My great grandmother, or maybe it was my great-great grandmother, was Indian. Or I guess I should say Native American."

The sound of Janie's stomach rumbling stopped him. He looked at her quizzically then raised an eyebrow. She flushed then explained that she hadn't had breakfast yet. With a gesture he managed to attract a waitress' attention and soon Janie had a menu in her hands. She was ravenous and only took a few moments to decide on an egg salad sandwich on sourdough and a cappuccino. She wanted to be sure she had enough room left for a piece of the lemon meringue pie she'd spotted in the dessert case. Dan didn't hesitate either, ordering a hamburger and sweet potato fries with a Coke.

She moved the flower vase to the side so she could see Dan's face, then filled him in on her news while they waited for their food. As she rushed through the explanation of her findings from the morning's search he listened attentively, never taking his eyes from her face. In her enthusiasm she leaned over the table and when she was done, she leaned back, almost breathless. "Well," he said, "I'm not a genealogist so I don't get where you're going with this but I agree you might be on to something. I think you should just keep plugging away. Eventually if we're lucky you'll find a connection."

Janie waited expectantly but the arrival of their food captured their attention. The smell of his hamburger was making her mouth water even though she rarely ate beef. Chicken was normally as far as she could venture on the carnivore food chain. She wasn't sure if she was salivating over the relishes and onions or the grease that oozed out of the sides of the bun as he ate. She breathed in the heady aroma and then got to work on her sandwich. Between mouthfuls Dan filled her in on what he'd found so far. "Okay so I checked into Rankin's story that he's investigating Clarissa's death. He lied. He's not on the case, in fact there isn't a case. No one in the Department is looking into it." "What?" Janie's hand froze, her half-eaten sandwich poised in mid-air. "How do you know that? Who told you?"

She forgot about her hunger and the food on her plate as she listened to Dan explain that he had contacts in the Department, having worked there for almost 16 years. He'd used his connections to ask about Clarissa. There was nothing going on. There was no autopsy in progress and no investigation. And knowing Rankin as he did, he wasn't surprised. Janie shook her head "I don't get it," she said, "What's he up to? And what do we do now? We need that autopsy to prove Clarissa was murdered!" Dan nodded. "I know, that's why I got one started. And I convinced them to do a toxicology report too." Janie sat back, stunned. "How the heck did you do that?" He grinned. "Let's just say that when I talked to my buddy in the Department about Rankin I told him that this friend of mine was gonna go to the newspapers and probably sue their asses off if Clarissa's death got ignored."

"Fantastic! Will you be able to get the results of the autopsy?"

"Yep," said Dan, "He's gonna text me and I'm hoping we'll know by tomorrow."

Janie smiled, then a frown crossed her face. "First I think it's Ken, then I think it's got something to do with whatever she was

146

working on before she died. I feel like I'm spinning in circles."
With a dejected look she sat back in her chair. Their waitress
approached to clear their plates and Janie pushed her half-eaten
sandwich away. She had no appetite now.

"It's too soon and we don't have enough information. You
need to keep doing what you're doing and I'll keep plugging
away at my end." Dan's words were encouraging. "I think I
should do some checking into Rankin. I never liked him when I
worked there and he gives the department a bad name. They're a
good bunch of guys but Rankin's a pain in the butt. He's lazy, he
doesn't follow the rules, and he'd sell his grandmother for a
buck!" Janie nodded but it was clear her enthusiasm was waning.
"What about Clarissa's cell phone calls?" she asked. Dan
explained that his buddy who could access those records
couldn't do it right now, so they'd have to wait. A sigh escaped
Janie's lips. "Just when I thought we were getting somewhere!"

"Hey kiddo, chin up. Why don't you head back and do your
magic genealogy thing, see what you can find out about Samuel
and Katie." He smiled at her across the table, raising his coffee
cup in salute. She smiled in spite of herself. "Did you just call me
kiddo?" With a grin Dan nodded his head. "You betcha!" Janie
could feel her spirits lifting. Maybe she'd just have a teeny piece
of that yummy looking lemon pie before heading back to her
hotel.

46

On the walk back, Janie mulled over the new information but soon found herself stifling yawns. Slipping into her comfortable lounging pajamas and maybe catching a 10 minute power nap was looking very inviting. *Face it, old girl, you're tired!* She was eager to check census records and obituaries to find out more about Kendall Duggan and Katie Donnelly. Those were all available online using her subscription websites so she could have a nap and then continue researching from the comfort of her room.

As she reached her hotel, she caught a glimpse of Morris coming out of the adjoining restaurant. On an impulse she hurried after him. "Morris!" She didn't want to shout but raised her voice slightly so he could hear. He turned but made no effort to stop so Janie was forced to chase after him. Out of breath and panting, she managed to catch up near the corner. "Morris, why didn't you stop? I haven't seen you around and wondered how you're doing." Janie's words came out in short bursts with deep breaths between.

"I know you," Morris muttered. "You're the lunch lady."

"Yes, that's me, Morris. The lunch lady." Janie repeated her question. "How have you been?"

Morris didn't answer. Instead he looked sideways several times and swallowed. "I'm going home," he croaked. "I just have to get them to give me my ancestors so I can get my money and then I gotta catch the plane."

Janie's heart sank. She was sure Morris knew more than he was telling her and that he'd seen more than he realized. She'd been hoping she could coax it out of him, given enough time. But it looked like her time had run out. "Oh, that's too bad Morris. I was hoping we could chat some more. Could I have a phone number so I could call you sometime and see how you're doing?"

Morris shook his head violently. "No! No phone! I don't like phones." Sweat started to bead up on his face and his skin took on an unhealthy sheen. Janie was alarmed and attempted to calm him but he had already begun backing away from her. "I gotta go," he yelled. Other people on the sidewalk looked at them and Janie tried to shush him. "Okay Morris, no problem. It's okay." He turned his back on her and rushed down the street. She sighed and shook her head. *So much for that lead,* she thought. *Time to head to the hotel.*

A few hours and two carafes of coffee later, Janie had quite a bit of information on Kendall Duggan but none on his mother Katie Donnelly. A power nap and coffee had rejuvenated her. Rather than use the hotel lobby computer and printer she'd taken the time to copy all the records she'd found and now her handwritten pages were spread out on the king size bed in her room.

Kendall Duggan began to show up under the surname Vrooman which was the name of the couple who adopted him in 1884. Using her favorite website Janie tracked him on every census from 1900 to 1930, then found his marriage in 1901 and his 1942 Draft registration. Now she knew that Kendall married and had one son Joseph Vrooman who was born in 1901 in New York. The 1930 census showed that Kendall had a one year old grandson named William.

Other resources provided Janie with the death dates of both Kendall and his son Joseph. A quick search of online newspapers proved fruitful and soon she had obituaries for both men. Joseph's 1982 obituary was a goldmine of information, giving the residence of his son William and the full names of both of William's children. Janie starred their names and wrote a hasty note which she covered with red asterisks and arrows, indicating that these were the great-grandchildren of Kendall Duggan, who was almost certainly Katie's illegitimate son Samuel. Katie seemed to disappear after the 1880 census and birth registration of her son, and Janie was surprised that she hadn't found a marriage or death record. *How could she just disappear like that?* Janie wondered. *And why leave her baby on the doorstep of a house?*

Sighing, Janie stretched, then gathered the papers into a pile. A nice warm bath might help her figure things out. She could relax and do some serious thinking.

Luxuriating in the heady floral aroma of her favorite bubble bath, Janie rotated her head, easing out the kinks that always came from hours of computer research. She slid further into the warm bubbles and was almost lying down when she suddenly sat bolt upright. Water splashed out of the tub with her sudden movement. *Chowderhead!* she scolded herself. *What a numbskull. Katie Donnelly was probably a good Irish Catholic girl. So if I find a church nearby all I have to do is look for the record of little Samuel's baptism and with any luck I'll find the name of the father!*

Toweling herself dry, Janie decided that if the catalog showed there was microfilm for churches within a few blocks of where Katie lived in 1880, she'd search the films tomorrow. To her disappointment the Catholic Church records in Manhattan didn't appear to be filmed. That was inconvenient but not insurmountable. All she needed to do was check online maps for churches near the Whitestone home that an immigrant Irish servant might have attended, then find out if there were baptismal records for May 1880. If she was lucky and found some, she'd call in a genealogy favor from a friend in New York who could go in person to check for Samuel's baptism.

Janie's cell rang as she was noting the names and addresses of the few Catholic churches that fit her criteria and had records for 1880. When she saw Dan's number she stopped and freed her hands to answer. "Thought you'd like to know that I got that list of phone numbers from Clarissa's cell phone the day she died," said Dan. They agreed to meet back at the cafe in an hour to go over the list. Janie's excitement rose. It seemed the pieces were falling into place. It was time to call her friend in New York with the names of the two churches she thought were possibilities for little Samuel's baptism. One more piece of the puzzle might be in her hands by tomorrow night.

48

Dan pulled up in front of Jones' Landscaping and leaned over to thumb through papers on the passenger seat for Ken's invoice. He figured he could get away with a quick look around by delivering his bill in person instead of by e-mail. With his head down he didn't notice the skinny greasy-haired middle-aged guy at first and when he did spot him, he quickly ducked down on the seat. *What the heck was a small-time thief like Seeds doing here? He sure as heck wasn't ordering any landscaping.* Something about Seeds being there made him uneasy and he didn't want to be seen by him. Seeds Hudson was well known to Dan and the Salt Lake City Police Department. He had a rap sheet about two inches thick. His nickname Seeds came from his habit of eating sunflower seeds and spitting out the shells. He left a trail of shells everywhere he went. He was a small-time crook who made his living fencing stolen goods. He'd also spent some time in jail for robbery.

When he was sure Seeds was gone he sat up. Striding to the front door he rehearsed his story in his mind. If Ken was there he was going to invite himself into the office, express his condolences and try to get a chat going. If Ken wasn't there he'd sweet talk the receptionist and see what he could find out from her.

Ken's office was as dirty and messy as it had been the first and only time he'd been there. The smoke-filled air stung his eyes and the smell of rancid cigarette ashes hit his nose the minute he walked in. It was pretty obvious Ken didn't care about the no smoking laws. They exchanged brief handshakes and Dan sat down in the cracked leather chair across from Ken. His eyes strayed briefly to the pile of sunflower seeds on the client side of the desk. There were probably forty or more in the stack. *So they're meeting for a substantial amount of time,* he thought. He wished he knew what it was about.

After submitting his final bill to Ken and failing at his attempt to engage him in small talk, Dan took his leave. It was almost time to meet Janie at the cafe.

Running a brush through her hair she added a bit more gel. Adding a touch of lip gloss finished Janie's casual look. She didn't have to think about what to wear; she'd just put this morning's clothes back on. She wasn't sure if she should take her laptop but she definitely wanted her notes to share them with Dan. Hesitating, she stood in the middle of the room, trying to think of all possible contingencies. Take the laptop or chain it inside the hall closet? Would she need it? It was awkward to carry with her purse and research bag. Shaking her head slightly, she made her decision and stowed the laptop safely in the closet with its wheely. Making sure she had everything she needed, she rushed out the door and hurried to the elevators. She didn't want to keep Dan waiting twice in one day!

Sliding into a booth across from Dan she fanned herself with the menu lying on the table. The heat was oppressive today and she wished the ceiling fans were going a little faster. "This is kind of becoming our hangout, isn't it?" she said after the smiling waitress greeted her. He smiled, and pulled out a sheet of paper.

"Here it is. All the calls your friend made that day" He leaned forward to point to the top number. "There aren't any names but we can start phoning and see who answers." They divided the list after their server had taken their orders. Between bites of her egg salad on wheat Janie dialed one number after the other. Beside each number she jotted down the name of the person answering. Her most successful ruse was to simply say, "Hi Becky, it's Susie." and wait. Usually the person answering would say she had the wrong number and then Janie would continue in a questioning voice, "This isn't Becky?" Human nature being what it is, most people would then provide their names with a "No, this is Sally. There's no Becky here." Dan's method was different but he was also having success and after each call he would add his names to the list.

Gulping down the last of his soda, Dan wrote one last name on the list then pushed it across to Janie. She studied it eagerly, hoping she'd see a name she recognized. Nothing jumped out at her. There was one entry with a single name and another phone number scribbled in Dan's hand. "What's this?" Janie pointed at the name. "I got this guy's voice mail and another number to call if it was urgent." Dan mumbled his answer after taking a huge bite of his hamburger. "But I haven't called it yet." Janie quickly dialled the number and was greeted by a woman's dulcet tones, "Mr. Whitestone's office. How may I help you?" Janie froze. She looked at Dan as if for help, her hazel eyes open wide. "Hello?" The secretary's voice sounded puzzled. Dan lowered his burger and looked quizzically at Janie while rotating his hand in a motion meant to spur her back into action. Finally words came tumbling out of Janie's mouth. "Hi this is Sarah Johnson. May I speak to Howard please?" A brief silence met her words before the response came "I'm afraid you have the wrong number. You've reached Andrew Whitestone's office." "Oh I'm terribly sorry!" came Janie's response. After a few seconds of apologies she hung up, a satisfied look on her face.

"Andrew Whitestone," she said, as if trying the name on for size. Dan cocked an eyebrow. He waited for her explanation. "Katie worked for a man named Whitestone, I'm positive that was his name." Janie's excitement mounted as she rummaged frantically through the jumbled pile of papers in her research bag. "There!" She turned the 1880 census page so that Dan could see it too. "Jacob Whitestone and his wife and son. He was the owner of the house where Katie was a servant." Her voice was growing louder and customers at other tables had turned to look. She immediately lowered her voice and continued speaking "And now this dude Andrew Whitestone gets a phone call from Clarissa the day she was killed? That can't be a coincidence!"

50

Dan pulled his phone out of his pocket and began searching. "Okay the area code for this Whitestone dude is New York so let's see what comes up." A few minutes later he was reading bits and pieces of a Wikipedia biography of Whitestone to Janie. It appeared that Andrew Whitestone was the only son of Arthur and Lillian Whitestone and a descendant of the American industrialist Jacob Whitestone of New York who made his fortune during the Civil War manufacturing equipment for the Union Army. The bio went on to state that Andrew was the CEO of Whitestone Pharmaceuticals, a New Jersey based company that developed, produced and marketed drugs licensed for use as medications.

They sat back in their chairs. Dan stopped reading and his brow furrowed in concentration. Janie's heart was pounding and the palms of her hands were clammy. *Pharmaceuticals! He'd have access to poisonous materials.* She shared her thoughts with Dan and he slowly nodded his head but cautioned, "We don't know yet that poison was involved in Clarissa's death. We have to wait for the toxicology report." Glancing at his phone he continued, "It says here Whitestone went to Yale. Didn't you say you saw a Yale ring on the guy who attacked you in the alley?" Janie nodded her head in agreement. "Wow. Dan do you think we're on to something here? I mean what are the odds? We've got this guy with access to poison, and he went to Yale so he could be Clarissa's killer and my mugger. Also he's descended from the guy who hired the Irish girl who had little Samuel in 1880! Is it possible there's a connection there? Clarissa had that birth record for a reason. What if Andrew Whitestone hired her to research his family tree and she stumbled on something he didn't want known. Like maybe an illegitimate child fathered by his ancestor?" Janie was speaking rapidly now, her voice taking on an urgency that surprised Dan.

"Whoa, hang on Janie. You're right about access to poison if that was the way she was killed, and also about the Yale ring but the rest is just guesswork. And I don't see much of a motive."

"Well there is something else. I almost forgot that in the birth registrations the father's name was crossed out but I could tell what some of the letters were." She rummaged in her untidy research bag, opening notebooks and checking scraps of paper for her notes. "Here we go!" she exclaimed while she pushed a copy of the birth registration across to Dan's side. "And here are my notes about what letters I think are visible, either b, f, h, k or l and then d or t. And Whitestone has an h and a t." Dan ran a hand through his rumpled hair "It's still just guesswork. We need proof."

Janie's voice rose. "If my friend can find Samuel's baptism record we should have more answers. Hopefully it will have his father's name. So let's go with this for now. If Whitestone is the killer could he get to Salt Lake from wherever he lives in time to murder Clarissa? And maybe he's the guy who was lurking around with a photo, watching her."

"That makes sense," Dan agreed. He might not have ever met her in person so he wouldn't know what she looked like."

"Exactly! So he'd have to get a picture of her somewhere. Oh wait I know. I bet there's one on the APG website." Dan looked puzzled. "Association of Professional Genealogists" explained Janie. "There are bios and photos of researchers along with info on their services. All he'd have to do is print off her photo and use it to find her in the library."

"Right. Good thinking." Dan was silent for a few minutes then added "It says he lives in New York City. So yeah he could get from there to Salt Lake in a company jet or maybe he's even got his own plane. Rich guys often have lots of expensive toys."

Janie nodded. "Agreed. And don't pilots have to file flight plans? Could you find out if he filed one a day or two before Clarissa was killed?"

Dan shrugged his shoulders. "Probably. Best way to do that is just drive to the airport and buddy up with the gal who works in the office." He gave her a wink and she laughed. "Okay I get it."

"One more thing," Dan said. "I went to Ken's office today so let me fill you in on what I found out." Janie's attention became fixed on him as he spoke. She could hardly contain her excitement. "Dan, that reminds me of something! I saw a pile of sunflower seeds on his desk the day I went there. It was the day after Clarissa died. So either he's a worse pig than I thought and never cleans his desk or this Seeds guy has been there before." Dan nodded his head in agreement. "Sure wish we knew what was going on," he said. Janie hesitated, then timidly asked, "Would it help if we had access to Ken's emails?" She waited for Dan's response. It was immediate. "Don't I wish!" Janie cleared her throat, "Well, umm I didn't tell you this before but I have his password. So we can have a look if you want."

Dan's eyebrows raised and an incredulous expression spread across his face. "You've got to be kidding! You could get into big trouble for that kind of thing." "So you don't want to look?" Janie asked.

"Are you kidding? Of course I do!" And with that he pulled out his phone and looked at her expectantly. Soon he was at Ken's Freemail account and reading the emails in his inbox.

51

"This is kind of odd." Dan pointed to an email that Ken had sent last week. It was addressed to studman@freemail.com and contained a brief note

Roses ready for pruning at 751 West Primrose July 3 – 10

There was no salutation and no signature. "There's a whole bunch of emails like that going to the same email address." He showed Janie. "See all the sent mail to studman? They all have a brief cryptic message that something's ready for pruning or weeding, along with an address and a date. Wonder if studman is some guy Ken hired to do some of his landscaping work or if there's more to it than that."

Janie nodded her head thoughtfully. "See if studman ever wrote back," she suggested. Dan did a quick search using the studman email address. Dozens of emails from Ken to studman appeared in the results. One email from studman to Ken stood out and Dan opened it.

Hey jackass what the hell kind of operation are you running anyway? The family was home you moron! It was a major screw up! Get your act together for next time or I'll find a new partner! Seeds

They looked at each other. "Any guesses?" Dan asked. Before Janie could respond he snapped his fingers. "Wait, we don't have to guess. We use the addresses and the dates and check the police blotter online. They publish their daily Watch Logs and that should tell us if anything happened."

It didn't take long to find the information. Each address in the emails Ken sent to studman had been burglarized sometime during the dates given in the emails. Each time the occupants had been out of town on a vacation. The only one that was different was the one that had caused studman to respond. That one was classified as a Home Invasion because the occupants were present when the thieves broke in. The police had no leads and had not made any arrests in the cases.

"Now what?" The frustration Janie was feeling was shown in her voice. "We have this information but what do we do now?" "I think I turn this all over to my buddy in the department," was

Dan's reply. Janie stopped him. "But won't we get in trouble? How are you going to explain us reading those emails?" Dan shook his head. "Not a problem. I'm not going to tell my buddy where I got the info, and he's not going to press for details."

He continued. "So it looks like Ken gives Seeds the info when his landscaping clients are out of town. That allows Seeds to burglarize the homes. And I bet Rankin is on the take and gets a little pin money from Ken to look the other way." He shrugged. "That explains Rankin not investigating Ken. He wouldn't want this little scheme to come out. So it kind of looks like we've still got Ken as a suspect for Clarissa's killer but now we've got Rankin and maybe even Seeds too."

Janie nodded her head. "Yep, if Clarissa found out about what they were up to, any one of them could have decided to get rid of her." She pulled out a notebook and started writing. "I'm going to mark down everything we know and everything we need to do to prove who Clarissa's killer is." With that she turned her attention to the notebook page, only looking up when their waitress returned to ask if they wanted dessert or coffee. Janie decided more coffee was definitely in order and gave in to the temptation to indulge her sweet tooth with a piece of carrot cake. Dan remarked "Well, looks like we might be here for awhile so I guess I'll join you" as he ordered coffee and apple pie.

By the time dessert and coffee arrived, Janie's notebook page was full. Dan had offered suggestions about what needed to be done and she'd added those, putting his initials beside the jobs he offered to tackle. They went over the list between mouthfuls of dessert and gulps of hot coffee. They agreed that they still needed to figure out exactly what Rankin and Ken Jones were up to even though they now had a long list of candidates who could be Clarissa's killer. Dan decided his first job tomorrow was to drive out to the airport and have a chat with the gal in the office, then he'd start following Rankin.

Janie decided to go to the library in the morning and hunt for more information on Jacob Whitestone and his family. She jotted down a quick timeline in her notebook.

Next she made a list of questions and a list of things to check. Studying the list and questions for a moment, she started a timeline for Clarissa's murder and the events around it. She made sure she noted every time she'd spotted someone watching or following them. There'd been the mugging in the alley when someone attacked her and the SUV trying to run her down might have been deliberate so she noted that too. Her list was growing long by the time she finished noting all of Clarissa's items that went missing. It was amazing how many oddities there were once she started listing them all. After completing the list she wrote down the names of suspects and together she and Dan checked off what motive, means and opportunity each one had. Whitestone was rich and he could fly anywhere at a moment's notice, and he had access to poison. Lots of means and opportunity there. But no known motive. Clarissa's ex had motive and opportunity and he also had access to poison.

Dan added a caveat "Just remember that sometimes separate incidents aren't necessarily connected." Janie was puzzled so he continued, "I don't believe in coincidences but it's possible that the mugging and that near miss in the street have nothing to do with Clarissa's death." Janie thought about that for awhile then reluctantly agreed. "I think they are connected but I see your point."

Dan checked his watch. "I should get moving if I'm going to the airport. I have to stop at the Hospital on my way to see my mother."

"Your mother?" Janie looked up. "Yep," came the reply. "Nothing serious but she's recovering from surgery and I try to visit every day if I can." Janie sat back, realizing that was why he'd been at the hospital the day she went to get Clarissa's purse.

Dan leaned to one side to get his wallet out of his back pocket but Janie held up her hand. "No, this is my treat today", she said firmly. They said their goodbyes and agreed to check in with other in the evening. "Will your husband mind if I call later tonight?" Dan asked. Janie explained that Steven was in Paris or at least on his way to Paris on business and she was on her own. His eyebrow rose in the quizzical expression she was starting to know. "Paris? That was sudden wasn't it?" She explained that Steven was often called away with little or no notice. His wealthy clients were used to immediate attention.

With a reminder to Janie to stay alert and be watchful, he was gone. She went back to her list, determined to note every clue, fact and question down so she could study it and create a plan of attack. She already knew what she'd start on tomorrow when the library was open but there might be more she could do tonight from her laptop. And she always worked better with a plan.

52

Katie tossed back the single sheet that covered her in her narrow bed. If only she could stay her with her sweet Samuel just a little while longer. He was only three weeks old but already growing plumper. She was glad she'd been able to nurse him properly. Mrs. Teadley was surprisingly good about letting her bring him to the kitchen while she worked and even let Katie take short breaks to nurse the baby whenever he fussed. Her usual twelve-hour days extended even longer now. The work still had to be done and if she had to spend an extra hour or two in the kitchen after everyone else was done, well that was the way it was.

She was upset that her lover didn't seem to want anything to do with her or the baby, and her resolve was growing to talk to him about it. She had to know that Samuel would have his protection in the future! A single Irish girl with a bastard child didn't stand much chance in New York City. Katie sighed and pushed back the covers. It was time to get dressed, change the baby, and get downstairs before Mrs. Teadley had a conniption.

Even though it was only 5 a.m. the kitchen was already steaming with hot air. All of New York seemed stricken with sweltering and suffocating heat. Katie wiped her brow with her apron and checked that Samuel was not too hot in his basket before setting it down in the corner. Her ma always said it didn't do a baby any good to be too hot and Katie was always checking the little one's face and chest to make sure he felt just comfortable. She had heard that over fifty people died a few days ago from this terrible heat wave, and many of them children and babies.

Her half-day was today and she was to have some time with Samuel's father. He'd agreed to meet them at the park shortly after 1 p.m. His wife was out of the city for the summer and Katie hoped he would spend the whole afternoon with them. She'd feel like a real family then.

"Girl stop yer dreamin' and get these linens folded!" Mrs. Teadley's voice broke Katie's reveries. She rushed to finish folding the table napkins as she'd been taught. It wouldn't do to aggravate

161

Mrs. Teadley today. Folding napkins was a time of relaxation for Katie. It allowed her to think about him, about her future – their future. She did love him, even if he had been so distant and cold to her lately. Her heart skipped beats and her face flushed if she spotted him even briefly. She hoped her little Samuel grew up to look like his father, tall and handsome with wavy dark brown hair. He was the first man she'd ever lain with and when she was in his arms she felt safe. Maybe part of it was missing her ma, and Joey being so far away. She felt so alone.

A sudden commotion jolted Katie out of her musings. Turning, she saw that Becky had dropped a large platter of ham slices which she was attempting to salvage before Mrs. Teadley noticed.

That was all Katie needed – Mrs. Teadley in a sour mood might make them all stay long past their usual time. Quickly she knelt, finger to her lips, and began scooping up ham and rearranging the slices on the platter. Becky followed her lead and began tossing the food back on the plate. Both girls gave the floor a quick wipe with the hem of their aprons and with the toe of her boot Katie pushed the last piece of ham under the butcher block counter just as Mrs. Teadley reappeared in the doorway. "Girls, what are you doing, Master is waiting for his breakfast!" Face flushed with the heat and a sudden attack of suppressed giggles, Katie turned back to her linens.

"Alright girl, you can go when those linens are put away. And mind you don't be late tomorrow morning!" Mrs. Teadley dismissed Katie curtly with a wave of her hand. "Thank you Mrs. Teadley." Katie smiled as she picked up Samuel in his basket and hurried up the back stairs. Once in her room, Katie tore off her cap and apron, tossing them on to her narrow bed. "Samuel you're going to meet your father today," she whispered. "But first let's feed you so you don't fuss, your father won't want to see a crying baby." Sitting on the edge of her bed, she nursed Samuel, stroking his soft cheeks and murmuring to him softly. "Sweet baby, I love you so much."

When Samuel fell asleep she quickly dressed him in fresh clothes then stood in front of her tiny mirror. The face that stared back at her was, in her mind, unremarkable. She inspected her face carefully. A spattering of freckles across her nose, pale skin, jet black hair so black it had blue tinges and blue eyes sparkling with excitement. Nothing to get too excited about, she thought. Quickly she pulled her long hair out of its bun and ran a brush through it, then tucked it neatly back in place. She secured it with a simple hairpin, then changed from her workday shirt to her Sunday best. She wished she had a nicer skirt to put on but her best brown underskirt with its matching alpaca overskirt would have to do. Her basque at least was form-fitting and still fashionable. She tucked the gold locket he'd given her deeper into her bodice, kissing it before she did so. Her secret talisman. She felt safe with it pinned to her chemise next to her heart.

Katie left the huge brownstone for her outing, her excitement propelling her along the sidewalk. It was hot and people looked miserable as they walked along, but she felt like skipping or running. The park was only about six blocks away but it wouldn't do to be sweaty and sticky when she saw him, so with an effort, she slowed down. She hardly noticed the people or the heat. Sammy was sleeping peacefully, no doubt enjoying the fresh air. Ma always said babies thrived in fresh air, it was being stuck inside that gave them the grippe and other diseases.

Breathing hard, Katie entered the park and quickly found the bench where she had arranged to meet him. He wasn't there and her disappointment cut like a knife. "Calm yourself now Katie girl," she whispered, "Just sit down and wait, he'll come presently." A half hour later she was seated on the edge of the bench, unable to control her nerves. Where was he? What was keeping him?

There! She saw him rounding the curve by the grove of trees. Tall and handsome as ever in a summer weight black frock coat, well-cut striped pants and matching vest. Smiling, she stood to greet him. "I was worried, you took so long to get here" She reached out to touch his arm but he pulled back and said coldly, "What do you want? I haven't much time." Bewildered by his tone, Katie hesitated, swallowed hard, and said, "I want you to meet your son. He's a beautiful boy." She lifted her hand to draw back Samuel's thin blanket.

"He's no concern of mine," was the curt response. His gaze did not shift from her face. Katie's heart felt like it was stopping. Her face grew hot with emotion. "I don't understand. Why are you *acting like this? You've been so cold to me lately and now you won't even look at your son."*

"For the love of Jesus, get to the point girl! I'm off to luncheon at my club and have no time for this nonsense!"

"But I thought we were to spend the afternoon together. You're acting like you don't love me anymore." Katie's voice quivered through her tightly closed throat.

"Love? Who said anything about love? We had a nice tumble a few times and that was it." Katie's pale face grew even paler and her shallow breathing was almost painful in her chest. Tears formed at the corners of her eyes and her lips trembled. "But we have a child, a son"

"I'm not interested in your bastard child."

Katie's horrified gasp punctuated the silence like a knife. "No, you can't mean that!"

"You silly feeble minded girl" he said, not bothering to hide his disgust. "Do you think I would ever leave my wife for someone like you? You were an adequate tumble in bed, not as good as the tarts on St. Mark's Place but all in all a pleasant enough way to wile away a few hours." With that he turned on his heels to leave.

"No!" Katie thought she was screaming but only a pitiful squeak came out of her mouth. She could barely breathe. "You will not do this to me! I'll tell your wife about us, and about Sammy. I'll march downtown in front of your precious Knickerbocker Club and yell it from the street. I'll tell everyone about us! Let's just see how you can get out of it then!"

His face darkened with rage. Grabbing her arm, he yanked her to his chest then twisted her arm behind her back. "You'll say nothing by God!" Spittle flew in her face as he hissed the words. "I warn you girl, you try anything of the sort and you will pay for it."

She'd never seen such fury. He frightened her, she'd thought her words would make him come to his senses but he was twisting her arm so hard she feared it would break. The baby! What would he do to the baby? Katie was sobbing now, pleading with him to stop.

As abruptly as he had grabbed her, he released his grip and she stumbled, taking hold of the bench to steady herself. "Why?" she hiccupped. Her sobs engulfed her and she could not get the words out.

Scornfully he stared at her. His eyes blazed with what looked like hatred. She heard him take a deep shuddering breath, then as quickly as he'd become angry, he regained his composure. His demeanor changed as did his tone of voice. He ran a hand through his wavy hair. "Don't worry, I'll help you. You won't want for anything." Saying this, he took out his billfold and stuffed a few dollars in her hand. "You and the baby will be fine." Reaching for his watch chain, he pulled out his pocket watch and checked the time.

"Now then, are you calmed down? Are you alright to go back to the house? I really must go but I want to be sure you're settled." He waited until Katie begrudgingly nodded her head, her eyes shimmering with unshed tears. A few moments later he turned and was gone.

With a moan, Katie sank to the bench in a crumpled heap. Her heart pounded, her constricted throat would not open for her to breathe and her chest and stomach felt on fire. Sobbing, she gave in to the waves of despair sweeping over her.

53

Darkness found Katie still on the park bench. She was exhausted. Eyes red and swollen from crying, she sat despondently, unable to function. Sammy showed his unhappiness with increasingly loud wails. Katie attempted to soothe him by rocking him but he would not settle. Pulling a thin sheet over her bosom, she offered her breast. She did not care if anyone saw them, even though she knew it was shocking to nurse the babe in public. His frantic cries stopped and he suckled contently.

Katie was dazed, her mind whirling. He did not love her, had never loved her, and she did not believe he was going to look after her or their son. It was up to her to make sure Sammy was fed and clothed and taken care of. She was terrified. How was an eighteen year old Irish farm girl going to manage on her own in this big city? She would almost certainly be let go at the big house. Then what? How could she get another position? The horrors of the Workhouse loomed. "Oh please God," she prayed silently, "Don't let me and Sammy end up there."

Suddenly Katie realized the sun had set. It was time to get back to the big house before hooligans found her walking alone. She'd have to think about what to do once she was safely in her attic room with the baby. Quickly she gathered up her belongings, tucked Sammy firmly into his basket, and hurried off to the main gates. She did not want to talk to anyone and hoped that Becky would not be her usual nosy self.

Sammy's basket swayed as Katie hurried along the streets. It was still unbearably hot. There were few people about, and those that did venture out on the streets at this hour were often unsavory characters. With relief she saw the brownstone just ahead. Going through the side gate, she made her way in the darkness to the servant's door. She stumbled once or twice on the uneven path. Without a star in the sky, the night was inky black and she had to make her way from memory. There was the door. With a sigh of relief she set Sammy's basket down and fumbled for the key in her pocket.

She heard a slight rustle and began to turn when, without warning, a strong arm came out of the darkness from behind her and pressed around her throat. A rough hand clamped her mouth tightly shut. She could not scream, could barely breathe with the arm choking her. She struggled, but her attacker increased the pressure on her throat. A coarse whisper came from near her left ear. "Stop struggling or I'll kill the child."

As if to make sure her assailant knew he was serious, his arm tightened around her throat and a knee jerked hard into her spine. "Do ya understand me girl?" His foul breath was hot on her neck. "Nod yer head if yer gonna keep yer trap shut." She nodded, desperate to breathe. His grip loosened slightly and gratefully Katie sucked air into her lungs. "Yer gonna come with me girl and not a word, not a scream, not a shout, nuttin'. If ya let on anything's wrong, I'll slice yer baby before anyone can help ya." Her captor gradually loosened his hand from her mouth and in a flash went to a pocket and pulled out a knife, holding it so close to Katie that even in the darkness she could see its outline. She dared not make a sound.

"Pick up the boy," her assailant growled. "Don't dilly dally! Give him to me!" He grabbed her roughly. He pushed her to his right side, pressed up against his body, and held the knife where she could feel it touching her. Taking the child's basket in his left hand, he shoved the knife in his right-hand pocket. "Mind now, I've got the wee lad and I won't mind slitting his throat if you try to run or scream." Shaking with fear, Katie did as she was ordered. Her only thought was to keep him from hurting Sammy.

They hurried along the quiet streets. To anyone on the street they looked like a young couple taking a walk in the cooler night air. Laughter sounded in the distance. A group of young men was heading down the street towards them. Could she cry out for help? Would he be able to get to Sammy before one of the men responded? Katie realized she could not take a chance. If she cried out or screamed, there was no guarantee any of the men would do anything. Even if they did, it would take them some time to react. As if reading her thoughts, he wiggled the knife in his pocket and drew Sammy's basket closer. He nodded pleasantly as the young men passed, one or two nodded back.

What did he want? Where was he taking her? If he wanted to rob her, why hadn't he just taken her handbag back at the house and gone on his way? All these thoughts flashed through Katie's mind as they made their way into back streets. These were rougher streets than she was used to, places where Joey had warned her never to venture into. Women dressed in revealing clothing stood lounging in doorways. Men of all types sauntered by, some boldly staring, others casting furtive glances at the women as they passed. Katie spotted some couples groping and kissing. Her captor turned down a back alley and she could smell the river. She stumbled but he dragged her along, never slowing his pace.

They had been walking for quite awhile. Past the docks, further down the river's edge, finally he stopped behind an embankment. The river was only a foot or so from their feet. Weeds and tall grasses hid the streets behind them from view. Katie closed her eyes, sure now that she knew exactly what was going to happen. He was going to force himself on her. They were completely hidden from prying eyes, no one would see or hear a thing. She decided that she would not resist, no matter what he did. She could keep Sammy safe if she did whatever he wanted.

Passing her the basket holding Sammy, he barked roughly, "Put the boy down." With shaking hands Katie set Sammy's basket on the ground at her feet. She prepared herself for what was to come. She started to straighten but he took her wrist, pulling her in tightly to his body, chest to chest. "Such a shame, a waste really," he muttered, and then the knife plunged deep inside her under her left breast. She felt a searing burning pain and gasped. Her free hand went to her ribs and she tried to hold the sticky wetness back. As he pulled the knife out another pain, worse than the first, struck her and she felt herself falling, her knees giving out. More pain as his knife fell again. He began dragging her to the water.

"Why?" she moaned. "Sammy...." She whispered with a faint breath. "Please. Not Sammy."

Pulling her deeper into the water, he gave a final push which she had no strength to resist. She could not catch her breath. She heard strange whistling noises coming from her throat. Everything was swirling around her, light to dark, growing darker with each second. She felt her heart slowing, beating erratically. He released

168

her and the dirty water closed around her. With no energy to lift her head out of the water, she tried weakly to grab onto him to save herself. But her flailing fingers grasped at air. Murky darkness surrounded her and with her last breath, she opened her mouth to scream Sammy's name. She registered an acrid taste of dank river water and then mercifully the darkness enveloped her.

Her killer stood knee deep in the water breathing hard. He was used to hard work but this had left him feeling winded. He watched Katie drift in the gentle lapping of the river, then turned and waded back to shore. Reaching down for the baby's basket he turned back to the river and took a few steps then stopped. This wee lad had done nothing to deserve death. He was an innocent.

All of Tom's religious upbringing had drilled into him that it was a mortal sin to take the life of an innocent child. The lass, that was different. She'd done a wrong to the master. What wrong he did not know but if the Mr. said she would bring harm to him or his family, that was enough for Tom. The great man saved him time and time again from the jail cells or the workhouse. He always did the Mr. favors when he needed help with such things. After all it would not do for the great man to get his hands dirty, no, that was why the likes of Tom Willett was around!

Tom accepted his place in life. He worked hard on the docks but the work was low-paying and intermittent. There was nothing steady to count on to feed his own woman and four snot-nosed children. It took a friend like the Mr. to make their lives tolerable. The extra money the Mr. paid him for rough and tumble work was a blessing and Tom believed not only in counting his blessings, but repaying such generosity as the Mr. showed him over the years. So he accepted, with only minor reluctance, the job of ridding the Mr. of a nuisance, the young woman called Katie. It was done and the $100.00 he'd been given in advance was burning in his pocket. It was almost three months wages and the wife would be pleased to have part of it. Tom had no intention of telling her the truth about how much he'd earned. A man deserved his pleasures and there was a tart who appealed to him near 2nd Avenue and 9th Street, and he meant to go back the first chance he got.

But the little one, that was different. The child knew nothing, it was not old enough to speak up about its mother's disappearance.

It was not a threat to the Mister. Tom hesitated, still standing frozen at the water's edge. No, he decided, it would not do. He could leave the child here at the river's edge but that held certain dangers. It might lead too quickly to the woman's body.

And so Tom, with his usual simple thinking, decided that the best plan was to leave the baby in a doorway. What happened to the child after that was no concern of his. He'd have done his good deed and not have to burn in hell for eternity. The decision was made. With a grunt and an almost imperceptible nod of his head, he wiped his knife free of Katie's blood, then turned away from the river and strode off with the basket containing the baby. He hadn't decided where he would leave the child but instinct told him to go as far from his own home as possible. And he was fancying a bit of time with that tart near St. Mark's place.

Thinking of the money in his pocket he looked for a carriage to take him the rest of the way. It was a long walk and a hot night. The air felt heavy and his shirt was already soaked through after dragging the boy's mother into the water.

After reaching 2nd Avenue he had the driver stop, then walked quickly over to St. Mark's. As he shuffled along he noticed a high-stooped brownstone house with a tin sign in German and in English proclaiming that it held a private school for midwifery. He glanced furtively up and down the street, and spotting no one, shoved the basket holding Sammy on the doorstep. The baby began to fuss, and Tom ran off down the street rounding the corner at Second Avenue before he could be spotted.

54

It was just past 11 o'clock. A young couple on their way home from an evening with friends walked past No. 76 on St. Mark's. A baby's feeble cry stopped them in their tracks. Another cry, much stronger this time. Heading for the worn steps, the woman spotted the child in his basket and picked him up to soothe him. "Oh Johnny he's so sweet but he must be hungry." The smell of wet urine stung her eyes making it obvious the child had not been changed in some time. "Ring the bell!" she whispered urgently. Her husband meekly obeyed, pulling the bell handle violently two or three times. Soon the door opened and in the doorway loomed a man, his eyes heavy with sleep. "A baby? On our doorstep? Well it's not ours and we don't want it! Go get a policeman and stop ringing my bell." With that he slammed the door in their faces.

With this dismissive response from the occupants, the young husband took his wife's arm. Against her protests that they couldn't leave the poor thing all alone, they headed off to the 17th Precinct Station house at the corner of First Avenue. Explaining themselves to the policeman they found at the front desk, the young couple soon found themselves leading the way back to the abandoned child, Officer Augustus Wiebe in tow. By the time they reached No. 76, the police officer's face was streaming with sweat. They could hear the child crying a block away. Officer Wiebe took the basket with the screaming baby back to the station house. There little Samuel Jacob Donnelly was arraigned and entered on the station house blotter by desk Sergeant Welsing.

Male child about 2 months old, found at quarter past eleven on Sunday night at No. 76 St. Mark's Place. Documented by Officer Augustus Wiebe

"Take him to Matron Webb," instructed Sergeant Welsing. Wiebe once more lifted the little one and carried him carefully to the top floor to Matron Webb. Samuel had now reduced his crying to sobbing hiccups when Mrs. Webb picked him up and rocked him for a bit in her arms, oblivious to the rancid smell of urine and feces that emanated from his clothing. "There there little one,

you'll soon be alright". Laying him back down in his basket, the Matron prepared a bottle of condensed milk as she did for all the foundlings brought to her. The baby wrinkled his face and fought the unfamiliar nipple but eventually hunger took over and he settled down enough to drink. After Samuel had eaten his fill and was almost asleep, she began to change his wet and rancid clothing. As she stripped off his little undershirt, an embroidered hanky fell out. Marveling at its delicacy, Mrs. Webb picked it up from the desk and studied it. The initials K.D were embroidered in a fine blue thread in one corner. "Ah little one, is that your name? K. D. I wonder what that stands for."

Matron Webb knew you could tell a lot about a foundling from the clothes it was wearing. This hanky was a fine specimen, better quality than the usual rags the foundlings had on. It was an Irish baby, of that she was sure. The clothing was of the type the Irish liked, and Matron Webb speculated that this child had an Irish mother who for reasons of her own, had abandoned him. He appeared well cared for and Matron felt a moment of sadness for the mother, then for the child.

Most likely the mother had born the child in one of the charity hospitals, then when discharged at the end of her two weeks stay, had not been able to care for the baby. A young mother could not work unless someone cared for her baby, and unless a mother could afford to hire someone, there was no way to do that. Many of the foundlings in the city were left by women desperate to find work and unable to do so with a baby.

Matron sighed and tucked the little boy in for the night. Come morning he'd be on his way to the Department of Charities and Correction at Third Avenue and Eleventh Street. Matron Webb knew that Sergeant Welsing was even now writing up the official request under Monday's date.

Police Department of the City of New York
300 Mulberry Street
New York, July 6, 1880

William Blake, Esq. Superintendent
Sir – a child is herewith transmitted to the charge of the Commissioners of Charities and Corrections
DESCRIPTION

Name unknown
Sex Male
Age about 2 months
By Whom Found: Mr. & Mrs. John Van Slyke of No. 112 Seventh
Street
When Found: Quarter past eleven Sunday night
Where Found: No. 76 St Mark's Place
Items Found With Child: Embroidered hanky with initials "K.D"

Signed. Officer of the 17th Precinct.
Sergt. John Walsing

The request would go with the little foundling first thing in the morning.

55

Mrs. Webb put in an uneventful night shift at the station house. The child slept peacefully and when 9 a.m. came, Matron called her assistant to take both the child and the request to the Charities & Corrections building. It was only a few blocks away and Miss Jennings was glad of the chance to have a walk. Picking up Samuel's basket, she headed out. "He's a good boy," called out Matron Webb. "Be sure you tell them that and mind you hurry back."

William Cronin, janitor of the Charities and Corrections Building, had a busy day ahead. It was his job to drive the van to the 26th Street docks carrying passengers for the islands. His wife kept a ward downstairs in the Charities building with seven cribs in it for foundlings rescued from the streets. Little Samuel joined three other babies already there. Their feeble cries filled the room. "Poor thing," said Mrs. Cronin to her husband. "I hope this isn't going to be like last year when we saw over two hundred babies through these doors! I'll give them their bottles while you wait for the papers from Mr. Hughes."

George Hughes was the Superintendent and it was his job to name each foundling and record pertinent facts on their commitment papers. Four sets of papers sat in front of him this morning along with the request forms that had arrived with each foundling. After glancing at each requisition form in turn, he assigned a hasty name to the first three babies – Annie Martin, Sarah Jackson and Emily Collins. Those he gave to his clerk who next assigned a number to each baby and made out one card for each with their number and new name on it.

Little Samuel's requisition form gave Superintendent Hughes a moment's pause. Based on the hanky found with him, this child had a name with the initials K. D. He should therefore be given a name with those same initials. Hughes could not think of a first name that started with K but then his eyes settled on the office safe where the name Kendall & Sons caught his attention. Kendall, he thought, that's a good enough name. His stomach growled and he wished he were already at Duggan's Bar having a beef sandwich.

Ah that's it he thought. And with a few strokes of a pen, Samuel Jacob Donnelly started a new life as Kendall Duggan.

The four cards with strings attached were then taken to Mrs. Cronin who tied the cards bearing their number and new name to the left arm of each baby in turn. The foundlings were now ticketed and ready for the trip to the Infants' Hospital on Randall Island. "Are you ready yet?" cried Mr. Cronin, thrusting his head in the door. "Yes, yes, coming!" answered his wife. "Here, help me." The babies were hastily picked up and carried up the stairs two at a time to the waiting van. Mrs. Cronin watched as each foundling was placed on the lap of a female passenger. The three abandoned girls were fussing, but little Kendall Duggan, held by a rather stern-faced older woman, slept soundly, blissfully unaware that he was now alone in the world.

56

Janie's cell phone alarm sounded at 6 a.m. She couldn't take a chance on sleeping in today since the library closed at 5 o'clock. She wanted to be in the lineup that was always outside the front doors before opening time at 8 a.m. As she showered, toweled herself dry on one of the luxurious hotel towels, then slathered on moisturizer to combat the dry Utah air, Janie went over her plans for the day. With any luck her New York friend would call with good news but she didn't expect that until much later, if at all. Meantime she could do some more research on the Whitestone family and on Katie.

She wondered when Steven would call to say he was safely in Paris. His flight must have landed by now but he was probably sleeping. With her time zone challenges she'd be lucky to figure out when he might call, so she'd just keep her cell nearby at all times. While she styled her hair and put on foundation and mascara, she decided it would be faster to eat at the hotel restaurant. She could get the buffet breakfast to speed things up.

With the window curtains open she could see the mountains in the distance and much of the downtown below. It looked like it might be a scorcher and Janie could see tourists already out in short sleeves and shorts. She'd better wear her beige capris; they were cooler than her black ones. A sleeveless blouse of cotton would keep her cool. Her red Naturalizer sandals would be perfect. They were definitely cooler than her running shoes. Tossing her research sweater in her bag, she strapped her laptop to the wheely, then slung her purse over her shoulder and left. It was 7 a.m. which gave her a good 45 minutes to eat breakfast. Steven would have been impressed!

Breakfast over and the bill signed to her room, Janie hurried out the back door. Even sticking to the shade of the maple trees lining the sidewalk, she was sweating by the time she made it to the library doors where she joined the lineup of other hopeful genealogists. She suppressed a giggle at the sight of computer bags, briefcases, research bags, and bundle buggies marking their owners' places in line. The owners waited in comfort in the shade out of the searing heat. At precisely 8 a.m. the doors were unlocked and the crowd surged inside to cheerful good mornings from the library greeters.

Last night she'd decided to look for Jacob Whitestone's obituary. He was such a wealthy man that he was bound to have one, and Janie wanted to know what his story was. She'd discovered that he was in the 1920 census as an 80 year old widower, but not in 1930. Her search took her to the online New York City death indexes for 1898 to 1948 and that gave her an exact date of death of August 22, 1922.

His obituary was glowing. Irish immigrant becomes self-made wealthy manufacturer. He was born in Wicklow Ireland in 1839 and came to America in May 1857 with a brother. He started a manufacturing company with a partner and made his fortune making equipment for the Union Army during the Civil War. He married an heiress named Augusta Culpepper, and had one son Charles Whitemore, and a grandson Benjamin. His wife died in 1892 and he remarried Sarah de Graff in 1894 but she was also deceased. He belonged to the Knickerbocker Club. Janie learned a lot about Jacob Whitemore but so far nothing was helping her connect the family with Clarissa's death.

She hadn't yet looked for a mention of Katie in the Missing Friends section of the Irish World published in New York. It was a popular newspaper column that 19th century immigrants used to hunt for other relatives and friends. If Katie had relatives in America they might have sent a query. A half hour later she closed her laptop and, with mixed feelings, sat back. It appeared an ad had been placed by Katie's brother in the Irish World and American Industrial Liberator in January 1881.

Sligo - New York City

DONNELLY. Information wanted of Katie Donnelly, last known to be working in the home of a Mr. Whitestone on 51st Street in Manhattan, New York City. She is 19 years of age and has not been heard from since June 1880. She may have an infant about one year old. Information thankfully received by her brother Joseph Donnelly 919 N. Marshfield Ave. Chicago Illinois

Janie's mind was whirling. *Katie has an illegitimate son, abandons him on the streets of New York City, and then disappears.*

It didn't sit well with her. It didn't make sense. Something was very wrong and Janie was going to figure it out if it was the last thing she did. Janie locked her laptop to the desk, threw her sweater on the chair to claim it, and headed off to the microfilm drawers. She knew exactly what film she wanted to check next.

57

Janie rotated her neck slowly and blinked her eyes. Scrolling through The New York Times looking for any mention of Katie was proving exhausting. And so far she'd found nothing. She knew the odds weren't great but she could never leave any stone unturned, any record unchecked, on the slight chance that something might be there waiting for her to find it. The ringing of her cell phone brought a welcome break. Other patrons scowled at her and she quickly answered, thankful that she'd tucked it in her pocket today.

Steven's voice sounded in her ear. "Hey hon, it's me. I'm in Paris and I miss you already."

She smiled. "Miss you too sweetie. How long do you think you'll be there?"

"I should be home in two or three days," was his reply. They chatted for a few minutes, then Steven ended the call with a hasty, "Oops someone at the door, must be room service, gotta run babe, talk to you later!"

Jimi Hendrix rang out again before she could put her phone on vibrate. More glares from others working nearby. Janie buried her head in her carrel as she whispered a hello. Dan's deep voice seemed to boom over the phone. "Guess what? Our pal landed his plane at Morgan County airport the day before Clarissa died. And it's still here." Janie closed her eyes as she exclaimed, "Yes! It's gotta be him! He must have flown up right after she called him." Dan nodded. "Yep. His plane's a Beechcraft King Air and I figure if he pushed it he could get to Utah in about eight hours including one stop to refuel in Kansas. I checked and his plane flew out of Teterboro Airport in New Jersey, so the timing works." Dan continued, "I also got a text from my buddy. Clarissa was poisoned. The toxicology report showed paraquat in her blood. You were right Janie. It must have been in her water bottle because according to my buddy, paraquat kills pretty fast if swallowed."

Janie sat back, relief and excitement flooding through her. "So that means something she said, something she told him she'd found, was important enough for him to kill her." She was whispering, wanting desperately to leave the reader area and go somewhere secluded so she could speak freely.

"Yep but the important part of that is that he's still here. That means you're still in danger. If he killed Clarissa because she found something he doesn't want known, he might think you know it too. That puts a big target on your back. That must be why he mugged you in the alley and he was most likely driving that SUV that tried to run you down. That must be some pretty damn important piece of information!"

"I think I know what it is," Janie's hushed tones were crystal clear. "But I don't want to tell you over the phone. Lots of ears here." A researcher in the carrel next to Janie shushed her and put a finger to her lips, frowning at Janie as she did so. Janie lowered her voice. They agreed to meet at the cafe in an hour. Dan wanted to swing by the library and get her but she refused. "I'll be fine," she asserted in a firm voice. "I'm quite safe here and it's only a short walk. I'll keep my guard up." He reluctantly agreed but reminded her that Whitestone could be watching her. Janie appreciated his concern but reassured him, "I know what he looks like now and I've seen him in two disguises so I'll be on the lookout. Don't worry about me."

Janie wanted to see if the attendant working in Lost & Found was the same one who'd been there the day Clarissa was killed. Library staff cut Clarissa's laptop free and held it there for her but someone pretending to be her brother had picked it up later. Janie wondered if the attendant might recognize the photo of Andrew Whitestone that she'd thought to print from the internet earlier.

Tucking her laptop under her arm and slinging her purse over her shoulder she made her way to Lost & Found. It was her lucky day because the same smiling woman was there to greet her. After a few minutes she reminded her about Clarissa and the laptop. The woman nodded her head. "Yes of course I remember that day. Such a shame." She also remembered Clarissa's so-called brother and was quick to identify the photo. "Yes that's the poor woman's brother. He was quite upset when he picked up her computer."

Janie tucked the photo in her pocket, thanked the attendant and headed for the restroom. She could hardly wait to tell Dan about this! No sooner had she gone through the swinging door when her cell began its song. She dropped her laptop on the couch that stood just inside the door and fumbled in her pocket for the phone. It was her friend Chris calling from New York. His search of the records of two churches near the Whitestone home had proved successful. Little Samuel Jacob Donnelly had been baptized on May 15, 1880 in St. Francis of Assisi, less than a half mile from where Katie lived. "And I got what you wanted Janie. The father's name is listed as Jacob Whitestone. Does that help?"

Janie sank down on the couch beside her laptop. "Wow. Oh wow! Chris, this is great, you have no idea how much you've helped. I owe you one!" With his usual foresight, he'd taken photos of the baptismal record and promised to email them immediately. They exchanged pleasantries but Janie's mind was elsewhere. Chris knew her well enough to realize she was distracted, so they said their goodbyes, promising to keep in touch.

58

Janie's hands were shaking with excitement when she returned to the reader. Her mind raced with a jumble of thoughts. The latest news nicely cemented her theory into place. Katie Donnelly, poor Irish girl new to America, gets a job as a servant girl in the home of the wealthy Jacob Whitestone. She gets pregnant by her employer, has his illegitimate son, then disappears. Janie was convinced that Jacob Whitestone had a hand in her disappearance. Did he kill her, or have her killed, or pay her to go away? She didn't believe he paid her to disappear, because if he'd given Katie money why wouldn't she have taken the child? A good Catholic girl wouldn't likely want it on her conscience that she had abandoned her child. And that could tie in to Andrew Whitestone not wanting this information revealed. It could possibly affect his inheritance.

Janie knew that the only way to discover if his illegitimate son was entitled to any of his fortune was to find Jacob Whitestone's will. New York wills were on microfilm and she quickly found the number for the one she needed. Minutes later she was reading his last will and testament which was written May 5, 1880 and probated August 27, 1922. Apparently he'd never felt the need to revise it. Janie was holding her breath as she read the legal jargon. There it was. Any children born to him were to receive 75% of his estate to be divided in equal shares. His wife was to receive the house in Manhattan and a yearly annuity drawn from her 25% share of the estate. Should any one of his heirs die before the other, their share reverted to the surviving heirs. That meant that little Samuel had been entitled to one-half of the original 75% of Jacob's fortune. Janie wasn't a lawyer but she was pretty sure that meant that Samuel's heirs would be entitled to a claim on Andrew Whitestone's inheritance. *And there's a big motive for murder,* she thought.

Forcing herself to slow down and focus, she took a deep breath. *Back to work, old girl,* she told herself. *Let's see if we can find any news of poor Katie in the newspaper. One step at a time Janie, that's how you always solve your genealogy brick walls, now use the same methods on this puzzle.*

It was almost time to leave to meet Dan when she spotted it. In front of her was a surprisingly lengthy article in the New York Times paper of July 8, 1880.

FOUND IN THE EAST RIVER.

DISCOVERING THE BODY OF A YOUNG WOMAN

A young lad out with a friend early yesterday morning stumbled upon the body of a young woman washed up on the banks of the East River. Constable Larkin, who was nearby on his morning police route, was called to the scene by the excited boy. Constable Larkin was able to pull the body on shore and secure it. Coroner Frost was then summoned to take the body to the City Morgue. A corner's jury was called to view the body. Dr. Wilson made an examination and found the body to be that of a woman about 20 years of age, 5 feet 5 inches tall with black hair. Three stab wounds were found on the young woman's back and breast. The jury rendered a verdict of death by stabbing and drowning by person or persons unknown.

The woman was dressed as follows: brown alpaca underskirt, matching overskirt with trimming, brown basque, gaiter kid boots, light brown lisle thread stockings, cotton camisole, and light brown gloves. Her only jewelry was a thin gold chain around her neck attached to a gold locket engraved with the name Katie. No purse was found but in her pocket was a brass key with the number 79 stamped on it. Coroner Frost, for the purpose of identifying the body, cut off her hair which measured 2 feet, 6 inches in length.

Murdered. Poor Katie. Janie felt sadness sweep over her. *What a sad ending to such a young life.* And no doubt her lover Jacob Whitestone had a hand in it. The list of clothing was not what a servant would wear while working, so perhaps Katie was dressed to go out, possibly to meet her lover. The final proof that this was Katie Donnelly would be to check the 1880 census page to see what the Whitestone house number was, to verify that it matched the key in the dead girl's pocket. Five minutes later and Janie had her answer. The Whitestone family resided at 79 West 51st Street in 1880. *So,* thought Janie, *there we go. This was definitely Katie Donnelly. Murdered.* She shook her head. There was nothing she could do about it. There would be no justice for Katie. But she could do something for Clarissa. She could, with Dan's help, find the proof needed to bring Clarissa's killer to justice. Andrew Whitestone, great-great grandson of the man who killed Katie, would not get away with it if she had anything to say about it.

59

The heat was oppressive but Janie hurried along, trying to stay in the shade as much as possible. Soon she was at the intersection and she stopped to wait for the light. The street was crowded today and she had to keep moving her wheely out of the way. It was so awkward for her trying to make her way without her wheely falling over or knocking into someone that she decided to hop on the Trax train for the next few blocks.

Bumping her wheely off the sidewalk and crossing to the train platform, she felt herself sweating in the oppressive heat. It wasn't long before she heard the Trax train coming. She started to move away from the curb but the strap of her sandal slipped off her heel, causing her to stumble. As she bent to fix the strap, she heard a grunt and was thrown off balance by someone falling against her. She thought she felt two strong hands push hard against the small of her back. Down she went into the gutter. Someone nearby screamed as the train passed only inches from Janie's head. As she turned her head in confusion she saw a man running and pushing his way through the crowd. She could only see the back of a blue hoody but suddenly she spotted Dan sprinting after him. Onlookers were helping her to her feet and she began picking up her bags and dusting off her capris. Her knee was skinned and bloody but it was only a little scrape. By the time she'd gratefully accepted a tissue from one of the women helping and cleaned herself up a bit, Dan was at her side, panting and breathing heavily.

"You okay?" his voice was concerned. When she nodded her head, he spoke in an urgent tone. "He got away but I think I know where he's heading. You up for a chase?" She nodded again and he grabbed her bags and wheely and began jogging down the street. "Then let's go! My car's back at the cafe!" Janie trotted as fast as she could to keep up with him, and they weaved in and out amongst other pedestrians. People turned, startled, as Dan jogged by and Janie had to suppress a few giggles at his repeated "Scuse me! Sorry, coming through!" as he passed. There were annoyed looks aimed in their direction, and she was pretty sure she'd heard a few cuss words from some of the people they bumped into.

Just when she thought she couldn't keep up the pace in this heat they were at his car. Even in her exhausted and excited state, Janie noted it was a dark red jeep with the top down. There were mud splatters in the wheelwells and dust and dirt partway up the doors. It was obvious this wasn't a jeep for show but for more practical purposes. She was snapped out of her musings when Dan threw her bags and wheely into the back seat, slammed the door and jumped into the driver's side. "Let's go!" he urged. They sped off as Dan explained that Whitestone had almost certainly seen he was being chased and would probably head for the airport to his plane. "It's about a forty minute drive so with any luck we can catch him before he takes off."

Janie finally caught her breath. "What were you doing there? I thought you were at the cafe!" "I was," said Dan, "but the more I thought about it the more I didn't like the idea of you walking over alone. So I decided to meet you and walk back with you. I was still a block away when I saw him come out of the crowd and rush at you. I couldn't get there in time to help but as soon as I saw you were okay I took off after him. But he got to his car and took off before I could catch him." Sweat was running down his face and he wiped it with his sleeve. "Oh yeah, and one other thing, he was driving a black SUV." Dan took his eyes off the road briefly to glance at her. "A black SUV?" She repeated his words as if not understanding what he'd said. "So he could be the guy who almost ran me down two days ago." Dan's only response was a curt "Yep."

He was driving like a madman, passing other cars and whipping back into his lane. Her hair was whipping around her face but the wind felt good after their sprint through the streets of Salt Lake. Janie wished she could calm her racing heart but things were happening too fast. "It was him wasn't it." She finally got the words out. Dan glanced at her. "Yeah, it was Whitestone," he said quietly. "You were lucky. I blame myself though for letting that happen. I knew you were in danger but I didn't do anything to protect you. I'm sorry." They sat in silence for the rest of the way, Janie hanging onto her hair with one hand to keep it out of her eyes, and clutching the door to stay upright as Dan swerved and weaved through the traffic.

Suddenly he braked, turned the wheel sharply to the right and pulled into the airport road. A few horns blared as they did so. "Wait here!" he yelled as he parked the jeep near the front door, jumped out and ran inside the terminal building. Ignoring his command, Janie climbed out and jogged after him as fast as she could. She was grateful for her early morning runs back in Trumbull, but wished she'd done a few more to be in better shape.

She caught up with him near an exit door. He was standing very still, peering out a large window at something in the distance. "He's gone." Dan's voice was calm and steady. Janie tried to see around his broad frame. "Gone? Where? How? We need to stop him!" Dan shook his head. "It's too late. He's taking off in his plane any minute now."

"What does that mean, Dan? Are we just letting him get away with murder?" Her voice rose. Dan turned, took her elbow and led her away. "No, but we can't stop him. It's time to turn this over to the police." Janie started to interrupt but Dan continued. "Hear me out Janie. We've both seen Whitestone in action. I saw him try to kill you. You can identify him as your mugger in the alley by his Yale ring. A library volunteer remembers him as the man who got Clarissa's computer by saying he was her brother. You've found proof that he had a motive for murder. We've got a whole stack of evidence pointing directly at him. So I say we turn it over to the police and let them take it from there. They're already investigating because the toxicology report showed Clarissa was poisoned. But they might never be able to put the case together that points to Whitestone."

Janie had to rush to keep up with his long strides. They were almost at his jeep when she put a hand on his arm. "Dan, wait. That's not going to work. They're not going to listen to me. I'm a nobody, just a genealogist from Connecticut. They'd probably think I was just a kook or at the very least, a busybody." She had his attention so continued, "You've got the connections Dan. You could take it all to your buddy in the Department. He'd listen to you. My flight home is tomorrow but I can copy all the documents that you need before I go, and I can type up a timeline outlining everything that happened before and after Clarissa's death. Then you present it to your buddy and just leave me out of it."

"You won't get any credit if we do it your way Janie."

"I don't care! The important thing is that Whitestone not get away with murder!"

"I think you're making a mistake but if you're sure, I guess I'll have to do it your way. "

Janie spoke firmly. "I'm absolutely sure."

"Okay kiddo, I can see you're going to be stubborn about this so you've got a deal. Now let's get out of here!"

As they climbed back into Dan's car, Janie looked at him and asked, "Did you just call me kiddo again?"

"You betcha." Dan grinned and winked as he put the car in gear and sped off.

60

"Constable! Constable!" The young lad's shrill cry cut through the muggy air of a sweltering city. "Here, over here!"

"What is it lad," boomed the young constable, sweating profusely in his hot black serge police uniform.

"The lady! She's all wet and muddy!" The young boy continued leaping over broken stones and dirt to the water's edge. There on the banks, half in and half out of the lapping water sprawled the body of a woman, her long dark hair drifting like seaweed each time the water lapped the shores.

Constable Larkin drew closer then took hold of the girl's shoulders and pulled her out of the water. He peered at the body, ignoring the young boy's excited babble. "I found her this morning when me and Bobby was up early for sumpin' to eat, she was just layin' there sir, all muddy-like and her dress sir it was up past her knickers!"

The Constable hastily grabbed the boy's arm to pull him back from touching the body. "Here now lad," he growled, "stuff it!" With that the young lad was quiet, but his excited breathing could be heard above the sounds of the water.

Constable Larkin knelt to inspect the girl's features. Her vacant eyes, once blue with life, now stared rigidly up at the morning sky. They were cloudy in death and her once-fresh complexion had a grayish-blue tinge. The constable noted that she had tiny perfect features with no blemishes, and had probably been quite a looker. Her long hair now matted and dirty from the muddy waters had been dark, perhaps even glossy black in life.

Although her dress was indeed up over her knickers as the young lad put it, her underpants did not appear disturbed and the Constable heaved a sigh of relief. Whoever she was, he was glad she did not appear to have been molested. He rolled her over gently, looking for any identification. Her pocket held a brass key marked 79 but there was nothing else, and she had no handbag. Perhaps she had one and it had disappeared into the river. He ran his fingers inside her bodice and touched something metallic.

189

Drawing it out he found he was looking at a gold chain pinned inside her chemise. A small locket hung from the chain. Peering closer, the Constable saw that engraved on the locket was the name Katie. Poor girl, he thought, pretty Katie, what brought you to this?

"Alright boy, time for you to run along home." Constable Larkin took out his police whistle and began blowing on it fiercely. He knew that other police officers would hear and come running. They needed the Senior Detective on this one to determine if this was a murder, accident or suicide. Poor girl she didn't look like a tart, more likely a servant girl. Could be she was in the family way, and jumped into the river to end her shame.

Her basque appeared to be torn and leaning closer he saw that one tear was stained with what looked like blood. He ran his hand over the opening, probing with one finger. He realized it was a knife wound that had cut deep. Sounds of running feet disturbed his thoughts and he looked up to see two of his fellow officers coming towards him. "Fetch Detective Jenkins would 'ya," he called out. "Looks like we might have ourselves a murder here."

61

Rain drummed softly on the roof of the sunroom. The paned glass patio doors were streaked with rivulets of water. Janie breathed in damp grass and earth, one of her favorite smells. She shivered slightly as thunder rolled and grumbled in the distance. They didn't normally get thunderstorms in August but today was one of those chilly damp days that foretold autumn's arrival. She turned the electric fireplace on and a cheerful warmth began to fill the room. With a contented sigh she sank into the comfortable shabby-chic green sofa. She loved going on a genealogy trip but coming home was always welcome.

Steven's broad frame was sprawled across one end, his left hand holding his beloved Kindle, and a cup of dark steaming hot coffee loaded with Bailey's in his right. The heavenly aroma of strong coffee filled her nostrils and Janie wished she'd made a cup for herself.

She worked her way carefully into the deep soft cushions, feeling her body slowly relax. One month after her Salt Lake City trip she was still recovering from the flight home and the excitement of Clarissa's murder.

"Mind if I watch the news?" She didn't want to interfere with Steven's pre-occupation of the latest book he was reading. He nodded then spoke "You've turned into a real news hound since we got back from our trip!"

Grabbing the remote she found half-hidden under the couch cushions, Janie quickly switched on the news. After a few minutes she heard what she'd been anticipating for the last few weeks. *"Andrew Whitestone of Whitestone Pharmaceuticals in New York City has been arrested for murder."* A video clip showed two detectives escorting Clarissa's killer, who was in handcuffs with a rumpled black jacket pulled over his head, into a building. Janie sat up straighter and listened attentively. Her breathing quickened.

"In a shocking development, wealthy New York businessman Andrew Whitestone has been arrested and charged with murder. Mr. Whitestone, the CEO of Whitestone Pharmaceuticals based in

New Jersey, was arrested by New York City police after an extensive investigation into the death of Ms. Clarissa Jones of Colorado."

A still shot of Clarissa flashed on the screen. *"Ms. Jones, who collapsed and died in Salt Lake City earlier this month, was a professional genealogist and researcher. According to Police spokesperson Sgt. Michael York, it is believed that Ms. Jones had uncovered information about Mr. Whitestone's ancestors that raised questions about the legitimacy of the Whitestone family fortune, which is valued at more than 500 million dollars.*

Police further believe Mr. Whitestone poisoned Ms. Jones for this reason. Mr. Whitestone is from the well-known Whitestone family who made their fortune in the mid 1800s in New York City.

Ms. Jones' death was at first believed to be from natural causes until Salt Lake City Private Investigator Dan Mulroney brought incriminating evidence against Mr. Whitestone to the attention of the police." Dan's familiar face replaced the still photo of Clarissa. *"Police investigators have confirmed that Detective Mulroney was instrumental in helping them solve the case. Mr. Whitestone is currently being held without bail. His arrest comes as a shock to his family and business associates in New York and New Jersey."*

Steven was watching intently, no longer lost in his book. "Wow Janie, a murder of a genealogist in Salt Lake? We were just there! Too bad you were running around chasing down an imaginary murder while a real one was going on. Did you ever find out what really happened to that woman at the reader next to yours? The one you were so sure was murdered?"

"Yes," Janie lied, "it turns out she died of a heart attack." Steven shook his head and settled back to reading. "I know how much you love your amateur sleuthing but you've got to realize that not every death is a murder."

Janie settled back and lowered her head so Steven would not see her half-smile. "You're right hon. That'll teach me to mind my own business next time!"

62

Janie shivered as she made her way through the long grass, wishing she'd worn her thick gray sweater on this chilly fall day. Her thin jacket wasn't doing the job. Thank goodness she'd worn her sturdy sneakers and not sandals. The grass was damp from morning dew, and sandals would have been a disastrous choice.

She glanced at the paper in her shaking hand, then tucked it back in her jacket pocket. E-165. That was the number the unsmiling woman in the cemetery office gave her. Now to find it. She studied each row as she slowly walked through the weeds.

There it was. Row E. She walked down the row, checking each small iron marker carefully. She reminded herself that each number she spoke aloud was once a living person. By the time she reached plot number 165 she was soaking wet from the knees down. She wasn't sure if she was shivering from the cold or the emotional impact of visiting Katie's grave.

She stood for a moment, studying the ground where Katie's body was buried here in Potter's Field. Ignoring the damp grass and weeds around her, she crouched and gently laid a bouquet of flowers on the earth. "These are for you Katie." She said the words out loud. She closed her eyes and continued, "I just want you to know that your little Samuel was fine. He lived and was adopted and had a good life." Janie's words poured out as if a floodgate had opened, and for several minutes she continued her story. "And you have descendants Katie, a great-great grandson and two great-great-great grandchildren. I'm so sorry your life ended too soon but you live on through them."

With one last gentle touch of Katie's grave, Janie stood. She took her cell phone out of her pocket and dialed a number she'd programmed in a month ago. On the third ring a male voice answered. Janie took a deep breath before she spoke. "Hello Mr. Vrooman. You don't know me but my name is Janie Riley and I want to tell you about your great-great-grandmother Katie Donnelly."

43692317R00116

Made in the USA
Middletown, DE
27 April 2019